Petals
from a
Rose

a Family Epic

by

Rita Louise Monaco

with

Janis Monaco Clark

**TURTLE
MOON
PUBLISHING**

Sandpoint, Idaho

Turtle Moon Publishing
Rites of Passage Books
Legacy Life Stories and Memoirs
Poetry

Petals from a Rose: A Family Epic
ISBN-13: 978-0-9913590-9-7

Publisher: Gail Burkett
Cover and Book Design: Laura Wahl
Editor: Janis Monaco Clark

Turtle Moon Publishing/Nine Passages
Sandpoint, Idaho 83864

Text Font: ITC Galliard 12/16
Headline Fonts: SimpleSnail/Ugly Qua

For my parents

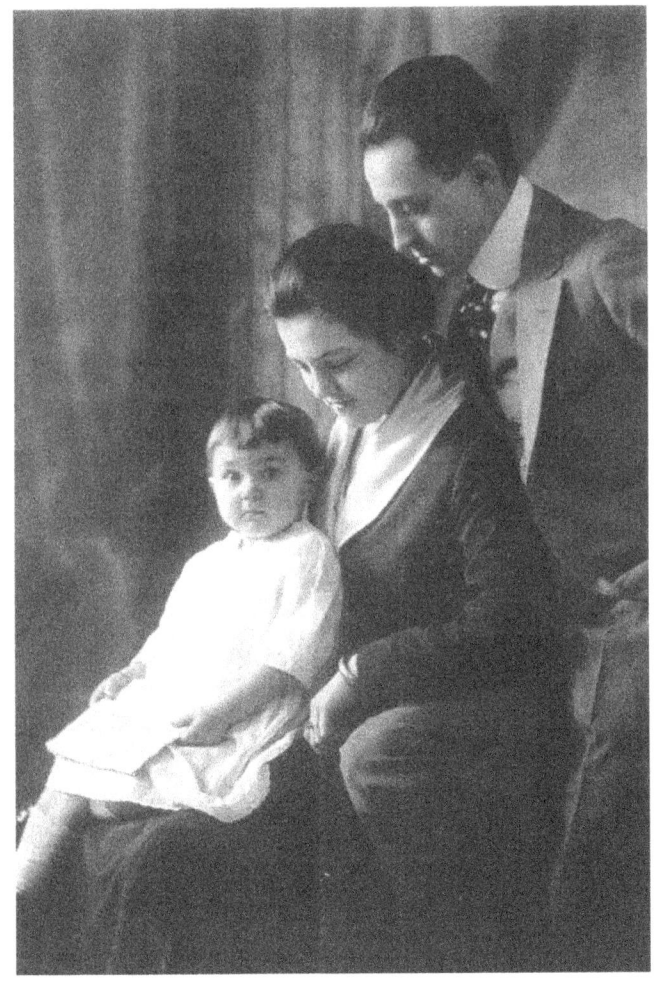

Rosa's hand in his had been soft and warm,
and as Paolo later told Luigi
"felt like petals from a rose."

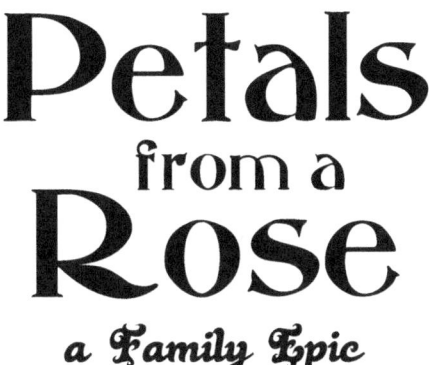

Petals from a Rose
a Family Epic

Table of Contents

Part One: ITALY   6

Part Two: AMERICA   78

Part Three: A NEW CENTURY   126

Part Four: GENERATIONS   160

Part Five: THE END OF AN ERA   220

Part One:

ITALY

CHAPTER 1

*S*equestered in the shadow of the snow-capped Apennine Mountains in the province of Campobasso, lay the tiny mountain village of Montelongo, home to families whose only resources were their meager farms, the fish in the lakes and inland rivers, and the abundance of the Adriatic Sea, where fishermen had toiled for centuries.

Along the banks of the endlessly pounding ocean, as if painted on a rough canvas, ancient boats securely anchored at nightfall, swayed with the rise and fall of white-capped waves. Seafaring men, both young and old, hands gnarled with the brutal onslaught of the sea, could be seen at eventide mending their nets.

A small fish-packing plant was situated not far from the docks and was the receptacle for the day's catch. Each boat was unloaded at the far end of the plant and the catch weighed on a scale that swung out over the dock. The fishermen were paid only a few lire for their day's toil.

The young children of Montelongo worked the farms while older brothers and fathers tended to the fishing boats. The only conveyance for travel, perhaps a mule, to carry a weary child back from the fields. The paths were long and occasionally a child tried to steal an onion or tomato, but discovery was frequent and the few cents earned were taken away; hunger amid such abundance was a mockery the peasant endured. No peasant owned land. They worked the farms further inland for wealthy landowners in a feudal system.

Under the mezzadria (sharecropping) system, a contract generally lasted three to six years. Crops were rotated in shifts of two, three, or four years, whatever the landowner preferred. For the most part, beans one year corn the next. The owner paid the taxes, defrayed the cost of preparing the ground, and provided the necessary implements. The peasant provided the labor retaining only one-third of the principal products.

Much of the work was done by groups of peasants who came down from the mountainous districts like Montelongo, permanent residence not being possible. The condition of the numerous agricultural laborers who were drawn chiefly from the rural classes showed proof of poverty. The terms of agrarian contracts or leases were in many regions disadvantageous to the laborers, in some regions, harsh, and in places absolutely miserable.

The year was 1866 and for nearly a century Italy had been going through the Risorgimento, the liberation and political unification of Italy. Vittorio Emanuele II was now king, Pope Pius IX was head of the Papal States, and Bettino Ricasoli, Prime Minster. King Emanuele was a small and insignificant man, good natured and shrewd, but superstitious and ill-educated. He possessed a rough-hewn but not unpleasant character; his enthusiasm was reserved for women, horses, and hunting. When his ancestral estate of Savoy was ceded to France, his first concern was the loss of his hunting grounds. Like his ancestors, he publicly maintained a mistress and illegitimate children, and seemed to think this was expected of a real king. He often told the silly story of how Queen Victoria's daughter fell madly in love with him, but knew too much Greek and Latin for his tastes. His own preferences were crude; he loved the simple people.

"Our king has a new mistress," announced the town gossip as she washed clothes at the river's edge with the other women of the village.

"I hear she comes from a poor family, but is a ravishing beauty," another chimed in.

"There are plenty of girls in the village who wish they had been favored by their king and could live a life of luxury," spoke up the first woman.

The women nodded their heads in assent and continued their babble over the new mistress.

The poor peasant in Italy who did not rebel had no choice but resignation to this life or they could emigrate. The motive was not simply land-hunger. On the contrary, sometimes it looked as though it was flight from an unyielding land. Deforestation and soil erosion were common. Numerous trees were felled and their timbers used for building and fuel. The practice of cutting trees to create meadows for grazing of cattle and to make room for vineyards, orchards, and wheat fields was common. As migratory shepherds drove their flocks to pasture, these animals fed on young beeches and chestnuts, nibbling at their leaves, stripping them bare or eating them away completely. As the small trees disappeared forests gave way to open meadows and vegetation was diminished.

Montelongo, where our story begins, boasted a small courthouse and also housed the local jail. A general store catered to the 320 inhabitants whose century's old stone dwellings dotted the countryside. At the edge of town stood tiny, green-shuttered, St. Anthony Church, a weathered cross hanging above the entrance its only adornment. Scarred wooden pews and dirt-packed floor appeared extreme in simplicity yet the peasants found comfort within the church's dim interior. The altar was covered with a clean white cloth. On the wall behind the altar hung a hand-carved crucifix, its features almost grotesque. Many a child or sinner shuddered at the sight of Jesus in his agony.

Padre Pietro, the village priest, carried out all the traditional duties of his parish. He baptized babies, married young lovers, and buried the dead. The good priest celebrated Sunday Mass and listened patiently to the confessions of his flock. Most of the peasants could neither read nor write; he encouraged the children to attend Saturday classes, but there was little interest in school.

The Padre was a small man with fair hair and deep blue eyes.

He tried without much success to tame his unruly hair under the hat he always wore, hopefully depicting a scholarly individual. He loved his parish and faithful flock and treated them with great respect, having come from a poor and loving family himself.

His best pupil was Rosa Costanza, daughter of Maria and Antonio, who had fallen on hard times. Antonio had worked in a marble quarry in the village of Spello, on a low flank of Monte Subasio, as his father before him, but he had been injured when a large block of marble fell on his leg making him a cripple for life. With no other skills, he was forced to do menial jobs around the village and this brought in so little money.

Maria had to take in laundry, a task she despised. She hated washing other people's clothes, and as she beat the clothes with a rock down at the river's edge, her tears mingled with the river water. Somehow, she had to find a way out of her misery. Rosa became caretaker for her four siblings, two boys and two girls, and had little time for studies, but Padre Pietro brought her books to read, which gave her much joy.

The old fountain stood as a sentinel in the town square, its water cascading over the stone steps as it had for a hundred years. Occasionally, a peasant dipped his hands in the cool water on his way to the fields, a respite from the oppressing heat. All summer long the weather had been unusually humid with the sun in its zenith. Blossoms that once graced the rolling meadow lay fallen to the ground. The air was so still that leaves on the trees seemed to be gasping for a cool breeze, but the cloudless sky gave no promise there would be any change.

A small dark-haired girl, perhaps twelve years old, hurried along a narrow path mercifully shaded by the olive trees that dotted the countryside. She carried a large piece of brown paper in her hand. She stopped momentarily to dip her hand in the cool fountain, brought a handful to her flushed face, keeping the brown paper high above her head so as not to get a drop on its wrinkled exterior.

"Rosa! Rosa!" called out a deep, masculine voice.

The girl turned quickly and ran into the arms of an old man.

"Oh, Zio! It's so good to see you!" The young girl cried out.

Her zio (uncle) was a shabbily dressed man, in the twilight of his years. His boots were covered with dust and a battered felt hat covered his graying hair. His hands were gnarled with arthritis and his gait was slow and labored.

The scene was one of great emotion. Rosa had always loved her uncle, his warmth and kindness touched her as no one else had. Her obvious happiness at seeing him was a joy to him. They tearfully embraced for a long time. He drew out his red kerchief, wiped tears from his eyes and blew his nose loudly. Rosa brushed tears from her eyes with the back of her hand and clung to her uncle's arm. The old man was reminded of his sister, Maria, Rosa's mother, whose dark beauty had enticed her husband, Antonio, so many years ago. Now it was Rosa, born again in Maria's image, but with a more enduring quality than he remembered Maria ever possessing.

Matteo stepped back and gazed keenly at the child. But this was not the little girl he had rocked to sleep, this was almost a young woman. She had a special softness in her demeanor, her eyes were large and intense, shaded by lashes so long as to cast shadows on her olive skin.

"Still delivering the ironing to the mayor's wife?" Matteo asked as he watched how carefully she protected the brown paper.

"Yes, Zio. Mama would scold me if I did not return the brown paper and string. Signora de Santis insists the shirts must be delivered in paper. So I wait until they give it back to me. Sometimes she makes me wait a whole hour just to be mean.

"Tell me, Zio, where did you come from this trip? Please tell me all, I want to hear all about it," she chattered on. "But hurry, Mama is waiting."

Matteo knew well the girl was expected at home to help with the chores. He sensed Rosa bore great resentment towards her parents because of all the responsibilities placed on her shoulders. For this reason, he made a profound effort to appear jovial, delighting in her laughter as he told her anecdotes he had picked up in his travels.

"Did I ever tell you about the farmer's wife who met me at the door with a pail of water held in her hand?" Matteo asked, laughing.

"No, tell me." Rosa smiled.

"Well, I suppose one of the pots I had sold her a long time ago was defective. One night after making a pot of soup, she noticed it had a tiny hole in the bottom and almost lost an entire meal," Mathew answered. "That pail of water was for me and she threw the whole thing at me," he roared, doubling up in laughter.

"Oh, no, Zio, you poor thing!"

"Yes, and then her husband came after me. I never ran so fast in all my life," he continued, delighting in her amusement.

As they neared the old stone house, Matteo could see his sister Maria at the door looking for Rosa. He had not seen Maria for six years and now as he neared the house he caught his breath in surprise, she had aged so and her hair was nearly white. The once handsome face was now thin and stern, her shoulders hunched over, calling to mind the burden she had to endure of too many children too soon, very little money, and a house too small for a large family.

"Where have you been, you lazy girl!" she screamed at Rosa.

"Aren't you even going to say hello, Maria?" Matteo asked. "It's been a long time since my last visit."

Maria was still scolding Rosa for taking so long, despite the girl's protests that Signora de Santis had made her wait so long for the brown paper.

"Eh! Leave the girl alone and come see what I have brought you, Maria,"

"Your dirty clothes probably," Maria said sharply.

"No, no, come see." Matteo handed her a package from under his arm.

"Well, what is it?" she asked suspiciously.

"Oh, Mama, Mama, open it!" shrieked the children excitedly, dancing around the table.

Maria opened the package, trying not to show any emotion. Inside was a small crucifix inlaid with mother-of-pearl. Rosa had never seen anything so beautiful and reached to touch it.

"So, another crucifix, and what am I to do with such a thing in this ugly place? Why didn't you bring a ham or food to feed these children?" she exclaimed in disgust. "Keep your crucifix, I have no need."

She turned away from her brother, hoping he did not see the tears in her eyes. Can't he see how poorly we live, her heart cried out silently?

She and Matteo had been the stepchildren of a wealthy merchant whose cruel disposition drove them both from a loveless home, she into the arms of Antonio, and he penniless into a cold world of which he had no knowledge. He was almost driven to despair and even attempted to take his life; his many failures took a heavy toll on his health. Only his love for Maria's children helped him overcome his despair. His meager income he gleaned from selling pots and pans to farmer's wives. He lived alone, traveling from town to town, a pathetic shadow of a man.

"Maria!" Matteo called, shaking her out of her reverie. "Let Rosa have the crucifix and I will take her to Mass on Sunday. Padre Pietro will bless it for her," disappointed Maria did not care for his gift.

"Yes, yes, go ahead" Maria sighed impatiently. Not wanting to hear more she went into the kitchen to prepare their simple supper.

Rosa was breathless with joy as she took the lovely crucifix to her sleeping cot and wrapped it in her shawl. The crucifix was the most beautiful gift she had ever received. There was very little beauty in Rosa's life, if any at all, and the possession of such a gift gave her renewed hope for her future. She had become weary of being the drudge in her home, weary of her mother's bitterness and constant badgering, and weary of her father's weakness.

There was never enough food to go around and she had to share her portion with the smaller children. She dreamed constantly of food and tried to imagine what it would be like to have all the food one could eat. Her resentment grew over the years, especially over her father's drinking, and it became more difficult to be kind and loving. She was a religious person in the sense she greatly feared the displeasure of God; she strived to lead a life free from any sins.

Rosa's greatest sin at this point in her life was that she harbored many feelings of anger over the demands of her family. Were Rosa's opportunities those of a well to-do family, she might have aspired to the position of a teacher as she had a quick mind and an uncanny retention of the written word. Her inward struggle against the bonds of poverty greatly saddened her. She prayed daily for an escape from her dreary life.

Matteo's visit was a happy experience. All the children enjoyed their uncle's presence. In the evening they loved listening to his stories, in the daytime he played games with them. To their delight he taught them how to build a kite. Because of the arthritis in his legs, he could not run down the meadow with the kite, but after explaining the technique to the oldest boy, he enjoyed watching the children run after their brother, shrieking their delight.

The tiny house could not accommodate another adult and, because of the hot weather, Matteo had been sleeping out of doors under a tree. This he preferred as he knew Antonio resented his being there and after a week, he sensed it was time to move on. Sighing heavily, his thoughts turned to the problems of the moment. His donkey had gone lame and he had been obliged to leave his wagon and provisions with the farmer friend who had given him the crucifix. The farmer lived ten miles away from Maria. He hoped to buy a donkey from one of his grandmother's old neighbors in Montelongo who might take pity on his plight.

Calling Rosa aside he drew her into his arms, "Rosa, I must go," he told her softly.

"I hate to see you leave," Rosa answered with great emotion.

After he had gathered up his few belongings, she accompanied him down the road for quite a distance, holding his hand all the while. They embraced, promising to keep in touch. Rosa again thanked him for the lovely gift.

"I will keep it all my life," she promised.

Matteo watched her walk back toward her home until he could see her no longer, then he sat down on the dry ground and wept. His tears ran unchecked, the events of the previous year flooded his memory. He had put aside enough money to purchase another small quantity of pots and pans to sell to farmers' wives on his journey, which he hoped would give him a new lease on life, but the memory of Maria's unhappiness haunted him.

The last year had filled him with great satisfaction and he had been eager to travel back to Montelongo. He had met an old farmer, Guido, who had lost his entire family in the great earthquake and asked for assistance in repairing the roof of his shattered home, which was caving in on one side. Matteo was happy to oblige. He slept indoors and the two of them could cook over an open hearth. He remained with Guido for more than a year before informing him he was ready to resume his journey.

"Ah, Matteo, I hate to see you go. You have been good company for an old man."

"I will always remember your kindness," Matteo replied.

"I have a gift for all your labors," the old man said. Reaching into a large chest beside his makeshift bed, he removed a cloth-covered article.

Handing it to Matteo, he said. "This belonged to my sainted mother, but all my family are gone, I have no one to leave it to."

Matteo unwrapped the parcel. The sight of the beautiful crucifix made him gasp in surprise as he realized its value.

"I cannot take such a treasure!" he whispered.

"Perhaps you have family you can give it to," the old man said softly.

"Yes, I have family," Matteo replied with tears in his eyes.

CHAPTER 2

The two men hoeing a large bean field made a comical duo. One tall and wide-shouldered, the other rail-thin and stooped. They worked in perfect unison, not stopping for hours. Gradually, the young man began to slow his speed. Leaning on his hoe, he gazed up at the clear blue sky. His shirt was open revealing lean muscle bronzed by the summer sun.

The old man beside him wore a floppy hat to protect his bald head from the sun's hot rays. What he lacked in physical power he compensated for with a great endurance maintained by sixty years of tenant farming. Like his father, Luigi Romano had cultivated the land for his lord. As long ago as the sixteenth century his family had sharecropped. In return, he was provided a pitiful house in which to live and a minimal portion of the harvest. This system created slaves out of the peasants who worked their lord's farm for a pittance, then kissed his hand and showed a groveling deference to anyone who dressed in a respectable way. While his master fed his dogs on white bread, the people lived on roots and grass.

"Paolo! Are you going to stand there dreaming all day!" asked the farmer.

"I'm sorry Luigi," Paolo replied. "I had a strange dream the other night and suddenly it all came back to me. Do you believe in dreams?"

"No, never," the old man answered as he spat on the ground. "They only give you fantasies that never come true. It's almost mealtime, so why don't we sit under that old tree and you can tell me your dream."

Luigi took out his knapsack and brought out some goat cheese and a loaf of dark bread. He enjoyed sharing his meal with

Paolo. He had grown attached to this quiet man whom he had found sleeping in his haystack four years ago. Paolo was twelve at that time and he too, had lost his family in the devastating quake. The boy was ragged and starving, his only food had been grass torn from the earth. Luigi had taken him in and fed him, then gave him his dead son's clothing to cover his thin frame.

They sat down together and Paolo began his recollection of the dream. He was aboard a huge ship and all the passengers spoke a different language. The waves were enormous and many people were sick. He tried to help an old woman but she brushed him aside. His eyes fell on a figure huddled in a corner and as he approached he found it was a young woman. Her dark eyes were terrified and her body so small and thin, he was amazed she could have endured the journey thus far.

Suddenly the sun had come out from behind the clouds, she smiled such a dazzling smile it awakened him. "I wanted to go back into that dream and find out her name," Paolo sighed.

'Well, now, that was a good dream," Luigi replied, stretching his arms above his head. "If I believed in dreams, I'd say it was an omen of good things to come."

"Do you really think so?" Paolo asked excitedly.

"Maybe yes and maybe no. Now let's forget about dreams and go back to work," Luigi said picking up his hoe.

But Paolo could not forget and longed to see the lovely face again. Perhaps I will dream again tonight and see her, he thought.

Many nights his dreams were terrifying in which he relived the earthquake. How well he remembered that horrible day. The earthquake buckled both ancient and modern buildings in cities that only the day before had snuggled quietly in a peaceful valley surrounded by snow-capped peaks. It also took a severe toll on castles and churches that dated back from the Middle Ages, including the bell tower of San Bernadino church from the 16th century.

Bloodied victims waited in the city's fields hoping for assistance, makeshift tents were set up, and soldiers distributed bread and water to the victims. Many nights Paolo's dreams relived the terrifying quake. His mother had sent him into the village on an errand and while on the road the earth began to roar. He was thrown to the ground by the great heaving of the terrain, giant fissures opened up as if to swallow him; somehow he managed to avoid the crevasses until finally the earth stood still.

Running as fast as his legs could carry him, he came upon his neighbor Russo's house, or what was left of it. Horrified, he stumbled on, passing farm after farm, each one leveled to the ground. Trees were toppled, livestock crushed. Coming upon his own house, his mind in a breathless whirl, he raced to what had been the front door.

Screaming now, "Mama! Mama! Guido! Alberto! Philomena! Where are you?"

The stone house lay in ruins. Buried beneath the rubble lay his mother and two younger brothers. Paolo worked like a demon to pull the stones off their broken bodies. Sobbing, he gently removed his mother, then little Guido and Alberto, and brought them out to the front yard.

"Philomena! Where are you?" he shouted. "Oh, God! Don't let my little sister be hurt!" he cried out in anguish.

But there behind the house, he saw a tiny white hand protruding from the fallen roof. Dropping to his knees, his fists clenched, he screamed obscenities to his God for the cruelty brought down upon his family. He dragged Philomena out from under the rubble and cradled her lifeless body in his arms. He sat there with his baby sister until his body became so numb he could hardly move.

With great difficulty Paolo dug four graves and tenderly placed his loved ones to rest. Papa will come, he comforted himself, he will bury them properly. Papa will do what is needed to make everything all right.

He lay upon the graves all night, waiting for his father to return from the sea. He waited six days, eating food he had foraged from his broken home. Papa will come. He will hear news about the earthquake and he will come home.

After the seventh day, Paolo set out for the village to look for his father. He met many of his neighbors on the road, all walking as if in a daze, some also looking for their loved ones.

"Have you seen my Papa?" he asked everyone he met. "Have you seen Dominic Cucco?"

How did Paolo survive? He had packed a knapsack with anything that was left in his mother's storage. After walking countless miles, he met a woman who said she had seen a man at the waterfront that might be Dominic Cucco. He was overjoyed, running until he felt his heart would burst.

Reaching the docks, he called out his father's name to all the men gathered there. None answered, while others impatiently pushed him away. Exhausted, after hours of searching and calling out, he fell to the ground. He knew that his father was gone and he would never see him again. There was no one left of his family. He was alone.

Cold weather blew in from the north and Paolo slept wherever he could find shelter. Finally, he found refuge in Luigi's haystack, and this is where the kind-hearted farmer discovered the half-starved boy who became his friend for the rest of his life.

Luigi had married late in life to a young woman named Anna Vito. She had been scorned by the village men due to a wine-colored birthmark that covered the left side of her face. But she was a good-natured girl, strong and capable. She had worked by Luigi's side in the fields and cared for their master's livestock.

Anna had a knowing way with animals. She made a creamy cheese from the goat's milk, the bulk of which she bartered in the village in exchange for staples such as salt and flour. She sheared the sheep, washed, carded and spun the wool. She had brought into their marriage her only possession, a loom from which she made their clothing.

Luigi's and Anna's union produced three boys who learned

early in life to assist their parents in the fields. The house provided by their lord was sparse. The floor was packed dirt and the only furniture were a table and five stools. Their bed was a mat made from wheat stalks covered by a blanket Anna had woven. The three boys slept in the loft on similar mats, with a large blanket that covered all three. A large fireplace, where Anna did all the cooking over an open hearth, dominated most of the front room.

Italy has acquired a reputation as being one of the most earthquake-prone countries in the world and the entire region where Luigi lived was on a huge faultline. The land was mostly a hilly terrain which produced fields of string beans growing up a small mountainside. When the earthquake rolled over the land, Luigi was alone on one side of the beanfield. Anna and the three boys were picking beans on the east side, at the foot of the mountains. Luigi watched in horror as the land opened the length of two hundred feet. Anna and the three boys fell into this fissure and were covered with great mounds of dirt that fell down the mountainside.

His anguish became a screaming hysteria and he ran for his shovel, digging frantically where they had disappeared.

"Anna! My Anna! My children!" Luigi screamed. "Who can help me!" There was no one.

Luigi remained in a state of shock for months. There seemed no meaning left to his life; he felt doomed to a lonely future. Fate intervened when he found Paolo huddled in the haystack.

Paolo was now sixteen. He approached Luigi with a plan he had thought about for sometime. "Luigi, I would like to plant some flowers, maybe some roses," he said, rather sheepishly.

"I have no use for such nonsense," Luigi answered quickly. Just as quickly he relented. "But it can't interfere with your daily work," he warned. "Where will you get the seeds? I have no money to give you for such foolishness."

"I can get some cuttings from the neighbors," Paolo said eagerly. "Salvatore assured me I could have as many as I wanted."

"Well, go ahead then, but remember what I told you about your work."

Every night after mealtime, Paolo worked a small patch of land, mulching and spreading manure until the soil was soft and aerated. He received slips from the roses of his neighbor, as Salvatore had promised. He discovered how to cross breed them until he achieved brilliant red and soft white blossoms such as never seen in those parts before. Luigi's pride for Paolo grew more each year.

Paolo loved the land. Many nights after sunset, Luigi would find him happily attending to his roses, whistling a song his mother used to sing. His whole body seemed to be in touch with nature, the animals and even the donkey responded to his touch.

Paolo was unaware of his good looks and when he and Luigi ventured into the village, young girls winked and smiled at him. He was extremely bashful and ill at ease with the opposite sex. He didn't dislike girls, he just could never think of anything important to say. He had no formal education, which filled him with remorse. He hoped someday, somehow, he would learn to read and write.

As he grew older, he became taller and heavier, and when he reached the height of six feet and three inches, his clothes barely fit his huge frame.

"How can we keep you covered decently when you won't stop growing?" Luigi growled one day.

"I'm sorry, Luigi. I remember my father was a big man, too," Paolo said.

He never owned more than one pair of trousers, one shirt, an old jacket and a pair of sturdy boots. He kept his clothes together by endlessly patching, placing one patch over another and so the people in the village gave him a name, *Ratto Pati Pantaloni* (Patch Pants).

Amidst the rubble of his broken home, he had found his mother's rosary beads. He carried them with him constantly, and even though he had long forgotten the prayers, the memory of his mother remained with him. Many nights she appeared to him in his dreams and he would awaken crying out her name.

CHAPTER 3

"Today I am sixteen years old," Rosa said to herself woefully as she looked at her image in the small, cracked mirror that hung on the wall. She was not happy with the reflection that she saw. True, she had beautiful dark hair that she plaited and wound into a crown at the top of her head. It makes me look taller, she reasoned.

Standing only five feet tall, she longed to be regal and poised like the queens whose pictures she saw in her textbooks. My nose is too small and my eyes too big for such a small face, she said to no one in particular. How can anyone say I am beautiful? Zio Matteo always tells me I am beautiful, but this you expect from a favorite uncle.

On Saturdays, Rosa took school lessons from Padre Pietro. She was an avid reader, consuming books until the good priest was reduced to begging books from the Franciscan Mission in Campobasso. She was the Padre's best pupil and he was filled with pride at the aptitude she displayed on oral and written tests. Her best subjects were Latin, Italian History and Literature.

Rosa's life seemed no more than washing, cleaning, and caring for her brothers and sisters. Her mother scolded her incessantly. "Why do you take so long at the river washing clothes?' Maria demanded. "Who are you meeting there?"

"Who is there to meet in this place?" Rosa answered, disgustedly.

Many times she would look about her room and begin to cry. She could not help but notice that great-grandmother's home was in bad repair. All the lovely old furniture was broken or scarred and no one seemed to care. Once she had loved this house for its antiquity, now she hated living here and longed for beauty. Her crucifix was the only beautiful thing she had possessed and she kept it hidden.

Young men ogled Rosa when she went into the village, but she treated them with disdain. One day a brash fellow shouted an obscenity at her and she beat him off with a staff she carried and began to beat him about his head and back.

"Mama Mia! Get this she-devil away from me!" he screamed.

"If you ever come near me or say those words again, I will put a curse on you," she shouted. It was an era when curses were greatly feared and the bully sulked into the village store.

"Better leave that one alone," whispered the storekeeper. "She could shrivel your manhood as you stand there. She has been known to carry out her threats."

Terrified, he ran down the street holding his genitals. The story of her recent curse was the talk of the town. One day, a group of farmers were gathered in the village store. Rosa was there buying beans and flour. The talk turned to crops and the abundant yield enjoyed by most farmers of the area. There had been a shortage of available labor to harvest the corn, beans and wheat. One farmer approached Rosa and said with a sneer, "Too bad your Papa is so full of the drink. He could have helped out and brought in some money for you folks."

Furiously, Rosa lashed out. "Mind your own business!"

"Touched a sore spot, Nick," spoke up another farmer.

"Who puts the old sot to bed?" Nick continued, enjoying the anger in the young girl.

With that Rosa turned her fury upon him and spat out, "May all your crops turn black!"

Rosa was not a vindictive person and would never knowingly hurt anyone. But when it came to attacking her family, she was beside herself with anger. Once said, she wished she could have reversed such a statement. But the harm was done and she fled from the store.

Whatever phenomenon brought about the disaster that followed will never be known. But the farmer's house caught fire and the harvested crops stored in the barn were reduced to black cinders. From then on, Rosa carried the unfortunate title of *malocchio*, "evil eye," one who could lay a curse on those who angered her. The folk of that era believed in dreams, witches, clairvoyants. And as in Rosa's case, the evil eye, someone who cursed those who opposed them.

Rosa ran to the chapel, falling on her knees before the altar and shed frightened tears. Begging God's forgiveness, she went into the confessional and blurted out the story to Padre Pietro, who assured her the fire was not of her doing. Rosa never forgot the hard-learned lesson. She tried to control her anger, calling on her faith to quell any unsavory words that might enter her mind. But the reputation as *malocchio* followed her while she remained in the village. People crossed the street when she came their way, an act that deeply saddened her.

Her loneliness and ostracism from the villagers led her to bury herself in books. Every spare minute she indulged in books of fantasy. She loved poetry and could recite from memory lines she found in *The Rubaiyat* of Omar Khayyam:

> *I send my soul into the invisible*
> *Some lesson of the after life to spell*
> *And by and by my soul came back to me and answered*
> *I myself am heaven and hell!*

One Sunday after Mass, Padre Pietro came to the house of Antonia and Maria to visit. Rosa was greatly embarrassed with the shabbiness of her home and rushed about, laying out a loaf of bread and a small piece of cheese for their guest. She was unhappy she could not offer him a glass of wine; whatever wine they once had was consumed by Antonio weeks before.

Over the years, the good priest had watched Rosa and knew there was little joy in her life or much promise of a good husband in Montelongo. He had secretly worked out a plan for the over-worked girl. A wealthy woman living on the outskirts of

Bartolemo had requested a companion. This he learned from Friar Bellini at the Franciscan Mission in Campobasso, who had asked for his assistance in granting the wish of the wealthy patron.

"She needs someone who will fetch and carry for her and run small errands, a young woman who is honest and reliable," the Friar explained. "Also, she must be able to read and write."

"I have just the person for you," Padre Pietro answered. "All I have to do is convince her parents."

"Is there a problem there?" the Friar asked.

"Well, when I tell them about the money offered for such services, they might consent. They are very poor." Padre explained.

"I will await your reply."

When the Padre first broached the subject, Maria was adamant. "No! No!" Maria shouted. "Rosa cannot go. Who will help me with the children and all these chores?"

Then Padre told them of the substantial sum to be paid for Rosa's services, Maria became very thoughtful. "That amount will be paid every month?" Maria asked.

"Yes, every month. Think what you can do with that much money."

All the while, Rosa had been listening. Her heart leaped in anticipation. Anything was better than the life she was living. When her mother finally gave her consent, Rosa ran to the room she shared with her brothers and sisters, and clutched the crucifix with joy. The crucifix had already worked its magic.

And so it was decided, Zio Matteo who had returned from his most recent travels, would deliver her to the Castello del Sole, home of Count Reno de Salvatore, to be in the service of his mother, Juliana. The only possession Rosa carried with her was the beloved crucifix. Rosa was never to see her father again, as it was not long after her departure that his body was found by a group of fishermen near the river's edge. It is believed he had suffered a heart attack, no one knows for sure.

CHAPTER 4

*R*osa and Matteo approached the huge castle with its imposing medieval towers. Rosa was terrified and begged her uncle to let her return home. But Matteo kept reassuring her he would stay until her audience with the Contessa.

"Oh, Zio, take me home please!" entreated Rosa, clinging to his arm so tightly he winced in pain.

"Rosa, Rosa, calm yourself," he spoke hoarsely, with tears in his eyes for his frightened niece. It was as though she had been sold into bondage for the welfare of her family. If he had the means he would have provided for his sister's family. But he knew he could not and brusquely asked her to behave.

Even Zio has turned against me, thought Rosa. I am nothing but a servant.

They were ushered into a grand hall the likes of which Rosa had never even dreamed. The floor was black marble and the walls were covered with rich tapestries. Statues stood everywhere, some so life-like Rosa stared in fright. From a huge winding iron balustrade in the center of the mighty room emerged a stately, elderly woman. She motioned for them to follow her into the courtyard.

What was to transpire that afternoon lived in Rosa's memory forever. It was as though she had been transported into another world far from the ugliness of her home. They had stepped into a fairy-land filled with fragrant flowers, and the sound of whispering olive leaves mingled with the cooing of doves.

"Am I dreaming?" she whispered to her uncle.

"Shh," he admonished.

They entered a white gazebo with seating that curved around the entire structure. The Contessa beckoned them to be seated, scrutinizing Rosa all the while. She was aware of the shawl the girl carried, holding it as though something precious was inside. Perhaps a pet? Juliana was not pleased, even though she was taken with the looks of the girl.

"My name is Matteo Totto, your Highness, and this is my niece, Rosa Constanza. I am sure the good priest, Padre Pietro told you all about her."

"Yes, he was quite extravagant with his praise." Pointing to Rosa's shawl, "She is not bringing an animal?"

"No, Your Highness. Rosa, show the Contessa what you have," Matteo instructed.

Rosa slowly drew out the crucifix, fearful it would be taken from her.

"And where would you get such a fine piece?" the Contessa asked with a trace of suspicion.

Before Rosa could answer, Matteo spoke up with great dignity. "It was a gift from me and has been blessed by Padre Pietro. We are poor people but honest." Rosa and Matteo were taken aback by this line of questioning. They stood up to leave, feeling they were not welcome.

"For the love of God, sit down!" the Contessa commanded. She liked Rosa's looks, and coupled with the recommendation of Padre Pietro, wanted to discover for herself the child's merits.

Handing a book to Rosa, she ordered her to read the first page. The book was *The Rubaiyat* of Omar Khayyam. She began, and in her melodic voice read slowly, with great diction, never hesitating nor mispronouncing a word.

To say the Contessa was astonished was to deny the sun's rising and she gently asked Rosa to read on. Rosa read the entire passage, stopping only then to look up into the eyes of Juliana. She was startled to see tears in the eyes of the Contessa who now spoke slowly and softly.

"Please, child, come and I will show you to your room. Signore Totto, be assured Rosa will have a good home here."

Getting up from her seat, she motioned them to follow her

back into the hall. Reaching into the purse that she wore at her waist, Juliana gave Matteo five gold pieces, explaining the payment was to be made to Rosa's parents.

"You will return the first of every month for payment. Please, provide her family reassurance their daughter is well."

Then leading the way, she began to ascend the stairs. Rosa gave her uncle a farewell embrace and followed the Contessa into her new life. In the days that followed, Rosa performed small tasks, writing short notes in her unique script for Juliana, reading long passages from such works as Homer's *Iliad* and *Odyssey*, and sorting mementoes into voluminous ledgers.

Juliana had her own private chapel and every morning she and Rosa attended Mass celebrated by visiting missionaries. Rosa was grateful for the familiar ritual and was comforted by the organ music and the chanting of the missionaries. She felt reassured that she was performing a good deed for her parents.

"Rosa," the Contessa announced one day. "You are in need of some decent clothes. Come into my sitting room, I have proper attire for you."

Rosa looked down at the dress she was wearing. It was patched and worn. She blushed in shame, "I am sorry, Your Highness, this is all I own."

Juliana laid out two new dresses, both black and extremely plain, a new change of under garments, a nightgown, and a sturdy pair of black shoes.

"You will change into these and we will burn those you are wearing," Juliana commanded. "There is a small bureau in your room that you may use."

Rosa neatly placed her clothing in the tiny bureau. Each night after Juliana retired, Rosa borrowed a small iron from the housekeeper, heated it on the stove and pressed her dresses. She kept her new under garments scrupulously clean, washing them every evening at bedtime and hanging them near the stove to dry. She derived such pleasure from this simple activity. She plucked a small olive leaf from the tree outside her bedroom window and placed it between the folds of her clothing. When she opened the bureau drawer, its fragrance greeted her each day.

Rosa took her meals in the main kitchen, eating only the food placed before her. One evening, the cook, Josephina, offered her a small piece of ham and a second helping of vegetables. Rosa's eyes filled with tears.

"If only I could share this food with my family," she said in a quavering voice.

"I know what it's like to be hungry," Josephina answered, clucking in a sympathetic manner. "Until I came to work for the Contessa, I was a poor girl with a big family to care for. There was never enough food to fill those empty stomachs. Now I can send the leftovers to my children."

Rosa never left Josephina's kitchen until she helped the good cook clean up at day's end. Josephina was grateful for the help and when Matteo made his monthly visit, there was always a loaf of bread and a bundle of sweets for Rosa's family.

CHAPTER 5

The de Salvatore family, originally from France, arrived in Rome during the seventeenth century after French troops sacked the city. Giovanni Damiano de Salvatore, with political connections to the papacy, amassed enormous property and wealth, marrying into nobility. Giovanni's great nephew, Count Reno de Salvatore, inherited vast tracts of land and family wealth.

Count Reno was a short, swarthy man, and if were not for his fine clothes, could be mistaken for a peasant. He had inherited his mother's dark skin, which he hated. He had gone to all the alchemists hoping to find a lotion to lighten it, but to no avail. His mother, Juliana Carancia, had been born in Bari, a seaport located in southern Italy on the Adriatic. The south was known for the darker skin of many of its inhabitants, who often were the butt of cruel jokes by their lighter-skinned countrymen to the north.

Reno's dealings with the bank of Rome were kept secret, only the bank director knew of his great wealth. He owned large herds of cattle and sheep and maintained a stable of fine Arabian horses. His cash flow amounted to millions of lire and he also hoarded great amounts of gold and silver; he would not share his fortune with anyone.

Reno loved the rewards of bringing to fruition months of surveying properties that were on the brink of foreclosure; he would never forgive an outstanding debt. Not only was he a shrewd businessman, but also the largest landowner in the region of Abruzzi. When he was in the city, one of his favorite pastimes was gazing out his office window, mapping out his strategies for the coming months. He was a hard taskmaster and worked the office staff mercilessly. The staff was not complimentary towards him, some even felt shame working for such a ruthless person.

"Another three farms have been taken over," whispered one of his three accountants to the other.

"When will he have enough," another lamented. "I hear he left the Martinelli family with only the clothes on their backs."

"I hear the old man suffered a heart attack, so great was his agony over the loss of the family home," the first accountant sighed.

"Yes, the young son has spoken of a vendetta to avenge his father's name," replied the other. The conversation ended when Reno came into the office.

Reno had also heard of young Martinelli's threat, but laughed it off. What could a young and penniless slip of a boy do to hurt him? He dismissed the thought from his mind completely. His meeting with the officers of Rome was more pressing.

Dante Damiano de Salvatore, Reno's father, had great pride in his three sons, Reno the only one with business acumen. He was eager for Reno to marry and sire sons to carry on the family name and fortune. His other two sons' wives had produced only daughters.

"You will be forty-five years old this December," his father reminded him.

"I am well aware of that," Reno retorted impatiently. And with that, he changed the subject.

The Archbishop's Ball, the social event that brought out all the dignitaries and their families, was on the calendar for the following month.

Guiseppe, Dante's old friend, called upon him and described the merits of his wife's niece, Constance.

"This girl is a real prize," Guiseppe boasted to Dante. Sixteen, full-hipped with a bosom to match. She has the promise of fertility in child bearing," he continued. "She will be at the Ball and we can introduce them to one another."

"She sounds just right for Reno," Dante said, as he rubbed is hands in anticipation. "I will speak to him."

When Reno was introduced to Constance at the Ball, he was greatly disappointed. Not only was she overly plump, but her skin was dark and matched his own, which added to his displeasure.

When questioned by Dante, who had noticed his son's disappearance after the introduction, Reno could only blurt out, "She is like a cow! Imagine the size of her in ten years!" He did not wish to offend his father by revealing his distaste for his mother's skin; he was ashamed of his feelings, as he truly loved his mother.

Protocol dictated that Reno remain at the Ball until after the banquet; he tried to conceal himself as best he could from Guisseppe and his niece. He was delighted his host had not seated him at a table near the offending couple and began to make idle conversation with the gentleman across from him. He was not immediately aware, therefore, of the stir at his right. Turning slowly, he looked directly into the delightful azure eyes of a young girl, perhaps fifteen years old.

Her skin was pale, almost translucent, and her face was a remarkable canvas upon which her aquiline nose was a distinguishing feature. Her golden hair was tied back in a large chignon, and tiny ringlets fell over her brow. She was engaged in lively chatter with an elderly gentleman seated to her right, whom Reno rightfully presumed was her father, Eduardo de Cordova.

Introductions were made all around and Reno discovered this animated creature was Elena, the Archbishop's niece, and this was her first Ball with "grown-ups." Her laughter was infectious and her bird-like movements were a delight to Reno. He was completely smitten and vowed to call upon her father at his earliest convenience.

Two months later a contract was drawn up between Signore Eduardo de Cordova and Count Reno de Salvatore, that upon her sixteenth birthday the marriage banns would be announced. Dante was indeed angry, first for having been made to look foolish before his friend, Guiseppe, but also in his son's choice of a bride. Disgustedly, he told his wife, Juliana. "She is thin and scrawny, she will never be able to produce sons."

Dante de Salvatore had reached his seventy-fifth birthday in very poor health. It was not surprising to the household when he suffered a massive stroke. His days of drinking and gambling were over. Juliana did her best to care for him, but she may have spared herself the trouble as he did not even know she was nearby. He died one month later, leaving several mistresses sorely distraught, as he had not provided for any of them. Juliana was secretly triumphant, feeling vindicated for the first time in fifty years.

It was the custom of the Italian culture that a widowed mother made her home with the eldest son. Reno insisted Juliana come to Castello del Sole to live with him. "We will have all your favorite things brought to the castle, Mama," he promised.

" I'm not sure your bride-to-be will want me, Reno," Juliana said sadly.

"Of course she will," Reno admonished. "You can have an entire wing to yourself. We will bring your own maids and cook, if you like."

Juliana took up residence at the castle, bringing all her favorite pieces of furniture, an antique armoire, which was a gift from Archbishop Scolesi of Bari, and a grand piano, given to her when she and Dante were married. She was glad her cook accompanied her, as she had a delicate stomach and could not tolerate the rich foods her son preferred.

CHAPTER 6

ount Reno de Salvatore was ecstatic over his coming marriage and began refurbishing his enormous estate. He discarded old, heavy ornate pieces and replaced them with delicate white chests inlaid with gold. Elena's sitting room was adorned with blue draperies. A thick Persian rug with delicate red roses woven on a white background covered the dark marble floor creating a dramatic flair. Precious Capodimonte vases, all in blue and white, were set upon every table and a white harpsichord stood in the center of the huge room. The walls were painted a soft blue and delicate chandeliers were hung everywhere.

Windows opened into a lovely courtyard which Reno had ordered his gardeners to completely replant. Every kind of flower and shrub had been placed in perfect symmetry. Olive trees surrounded the courtyard; brilliant red bougainvillea and jasmine were trained over countless trellises making the entire area one of great beauty. Marble statues of angels and cherubs were interspersed with the trellises and a pink marble fountain with white doves stood in the center of it all. Reno had an aviary built in one section of the courtyard and imported birds of every color and many species to lodge amidst brilliant foliage. All his endeavors were truly an act of fascination for the girl who was to become his wife.

The happy day arrived and even Juliana had to grudgingly admit, in spite of Dante's remarks, that Elena was a radiant bride. Her gown was exquisitely fashioned of the finest Venetian lace, the entire bodice covered with dainty seed pearls. The headdress was a tiny crown of similar seed pearls and to this was attached a long, flowing veil that billowed softly behind her.

Reno had presented her with a diamond and ruby engagement ring set on a wide gold band. Her wedding ring consisted of four large diamonds; guests were astonished by the grand display of wealth. Every flower for miles had been transported in huge white baskets.

Rich tapestries adorned the walls of the Basillica de Santo Paolo and a fine Chinese silk carpet extended the entire length of the church for Elena's walk down the aisle. Reno's happiness knew no bounds when he saw her appear on her father's arm, stepping daintily to the music of the great organ.

Archbishop Scolesi performed the ceremony, praying in his heart Elena would settle down and become a good wife. Elena was his deceased sister's only child and his eyes filled with tears of gladness. The feast that followed was one the townspeople never tired of describing. Wine flowed like water and the guests danced until early morning.

Reno bedded his wife and was a gentle, loving husband. But Elena was revolted by her husband's love-making. Many nights she thwarted his amorous advances with complaints of fatigue. Perhaps, had she been more receptive, she would have been happier; it may have softened her personality. Instead, she was prone to offer complaints more often than praise.

"I need a new side-saddle, it is very difficult riding with your huge horses," she would complain.

"The dinner was too heavy, all salt and too spicy. I have a terrible stomach ache!"

She found she received a huge allowance to spend on anything she chose, but most importantly, she was now nobility.

Elena's mother had died when the child was two years old. From that time on, Elena became the queen of the household, badly spoiled by her doting father. She had learned early in life to wheedle and cajole her proud father. Her tantrums were feared by the servants as she was permitted to dismiss anyone who displeased her. Her demands were great and her displeasures many.

"Such a bad seed," whispered the servants to one another. "How can anyone with fine privileges have such a bad heart?"

"Tis sad the Master did not have a son instead of that one," the servants complained.

Elena had been a rebellious child, and even though her father had sent her to the finest schools in Switzerland, her mischievous ways were a bane to her teachers. In one instance she and her girl friend, Carmela, set fire to the chemistry workroom and then tried to cover up their crime with the excuse it was only because of an experiment with dangerous chemicals.

The headmistress was not to be fooled, however, and Elena was sent to the Immaculate Conception Convent in Rome at the request of her uncle, Archbishop Scolesi. But the good sisters of the convent were at their wits end in their attempts to school such a rebel.

"What are we to do, Mother?" Sister Bernadette asked Mother Superior. "She is too much for us to handle. We wish for her to leave." Mother Superior agreed.

The child disrupted the entire convent and so she was sent home, much to the Sisters' embarrassment; Archbishop Scolesi was a good friend and generous contributor to the convent. Eduardo was greatly offended and decided his daughter did not need any more schooling, her beauty assured him she would make a good marriage. Indeed, Elena's marriage to the Count proved he was right. She was now Contessa de Castello del Sole, a role she greatly flaunted.

CHAPTER 7

In the following months Contessa Juliana did not intrude in the main rooms of the castle where Reno and Elena dwelt. She only appeared when she was invited for a special occasion. Elena did not want to socialize with Juliana, whom she felt was far too strict and old-fashioned.

Juliana believed that a wife was beholden to her husband. Every woman's role was to bear sons and do all she could to further her husband's ambitions. Juliana was perceptive. She saw Elena's false ways behind her façade of dainty innocence. She worried that Reno, in time, would have a troublesome marriage.

In the meantime, Rosa and Juliana had established a warm relationship. Juliana had given birth to three sons and had always longed for a daughter. There was no warmth between she and Elena, much to the older woman's regret, perhaps it was because Elena never knew her mother. Juliana longed to give something of her own mother's jewelry to Elena, but was sure it could never measure up to the fine pieces Reno showered upon his adored wife.

Juliana was aware of the crucifix Rosa guarded so carefully, and treasured so. Going through the treasure chest that belonged to her cherished mother, Luisa, she came upon a small broach, hidden in its recesses; she had given it to her mother on her birthday. Tearfully, she wrapped it in a silk scarf to offer to Rosa, as a token of her warmth toward the young girl.

Juliana smiled and held out the wrapped gift. "Rosa, I have a small gift in appreciation for your labors."

Unwrapping the scarf, tears filled Rosa's dark eyes as she attempted to thank her benefactress.

"Here, let me pin it on your dress," Juliana whispered with a smile. From that day on, theirs was a warm relationship, almost as much as family.

Time passed slowly for Reno. He had anticipated that because Elena was a young, healthy female she would be in the family way in a very short time. He was deeply distraught, thinking it caused his adored pain. He could not see her unhappy as she had enriched his life with her animation and spirited ways. He delighted in bringing her expensive gifts and ever-searching for some new bauble to please her. It was on one of his many trips that he heard of a man who grew splendid roses of such color and variety that he vowed he would bring these flowers to his beloved.

It was learned in Luigi's village of Lucera, that a powerful and wealthy Count was searching for the "Rose Man." The only such person the villagers knew of was Paolo, so word was sent by messenger to Count Reno of Paolo's whereabouts.

One day a fine carriage carrying Reno and Elena, drawn by two magnificent white horses, appeared in the village. The mayor, greatly flustered by such royalty, proceeded to apologize for the poor condition of the roads.

Arriving at the farmhouse, Elena insisted on being escorted immediately to the rose garden. Her exclamations of delight were music to Reno's ears. Paolo stood shyly by, answering all the Count's questions as best he could. He had never been in the company of nobility and was greatly ashamed of his patched pants and clumsy boots. Nevertheless, his heart swelled with pride for not ever in his young life had he heard such words of praise. His eyes shone with pleasure and he spoke in a quiet voice.

Elena anticipated the "Rose Man" to be a simple peasant, but was taken aback by the strong, handsome man before her. Her heart beat loudly in her breast and she tried to conceal the excitement that flowed through her body.

"Paolo, could you accompany us back to Castello del Sole and explain to our gardeners how to care for your roses?" the Count asked.

Paolo looked to Luigi for an answer.

"My son will be happy to be of service, Your Highness," Luigi answered, bowing low.

Puzzled, Paolo took Luigi aside and exclaimed, "Luigi, who is this son you are talking about?"

"You, of course, you fool," Luigi shot back. "You have been a son to me ever since you slept in my haystack."

"I cannot leave you, old man. This is my home."

"This is an opportunity of a lifetime," Luigi said in exasperation. "Go, and if you are truly unhappy you can always return. It is time for you to spread your wings and fly to another place."

Tears came into the eyes of the old man, which he wiped away with the back of his hand. What would life be without Paolo? But he could not stand in the way of such a grand opportunity. This could be the turning point in the young man's life.

Carefully taking slips from all the roses and wrapping them in large wet leaves, Paolo mounted a burro provided for him and set off to a new adventure. There was no need to pack a bag, he only possessed the clothes on his back. He kept looking over his shoulder toward Luigi until the old farmer was out of his sight. He could never repay Luigi for all he had done for him and he vowed that someday he would make a home for his old friend.

CHAPTER 8

*P*aolo had lived a simple life and the enormity and richness of Castello del Sole overwhelmed him. So many workers confused him. There were scullery maids, gardeners, blacksmiths, carpenters, stable hands and many cooks. He was given a cot behind the huge stable. It was dry and warm there and he could smell and hear the magnificent stallions housed nearby in the next building.

Life at the estate was not all he had anticipated. The other gardeners were envious of his way with the roses and ridiculed his poor clothing. They did everything to make his life miserable, tearing up his shoots, pouring salt into the soil, until Paolo was forced to sleep in the rose garden, guarding it from their treachery. He was not happy with this turn of events.

It was here Elena found him one morning, asleep beside a particularly fine rose bush, one of Elena's favorites. Seeing his strong body she ached to be near him. Many nights since his arrival, she lay awake imagining him making passionate love to her. She dreamed of his splendid body beside her, all the time disgusted with Reno's presence in her bed. In her dreams, Paolo's strong hands caressed her breasts and his lips were hot and moist against her skin.

Paolo was so distraught over the loss of his roses that he nervously conveyed this to Elena. "I am sorry, Your Highness, but the other gardeners have destroyed some of the rose bushes and I must guard them against their attacks."

"How terrible! I must talk with the Count," Elena said in an angry voice, and off she went to find Reno. Upon learning of the destruction of the rose bushes, Reno without hesitation dismissed all the gardeners.

Turning to Paolo, he said, "Who shall we get to replace them?"

"Luigi could be my helper, Your Highness," Paolo replied without hesitation.

"Can the two of you handle this place yourselves?" Reno asked.

"Yes, I know we can," Paolo answered eagerly. "We cared for a large farm by ourselves."

Luigi had been a tenant farmer all his life and when he received word he could be with Paolo at the castle, he gleefully left the old farm. He was ready for a new adventure, too. He and Paolo were together again.

Upon arriving at Castello del Sole, however, Luigi noticed something that he could not dismiss lightly. He suspected that Elena hoped to find Paolo alone in the rose garden for he could see the desire in her eyes when she looked at the tall, handsome man. Luigi was alert and watched her whenever she appeared.

CHAPTER 9

*V*ito Martinelli had been a good son, caring for his aged mother since the death of his father many years ago. He provided her with a small house, and because she was confined to a wheelchair, he had hired a young girl to live-in and care for her. Every month he visited his mother, bringing the fruit and vegetables that she loved.

"Vito, my son, it is so good to see you. You are looking unusually well," she exclaimed as he leaned down to kiss her. She could see the happiness on his face and his eyes had a brightness she had never seen.

"Mama, we at last will have our vendetta," Vito whispered in a husky voice.

"Ah, my son why do you live in the past? What is done, is done, God will punish him," but she had great fear in her voice.

"Never! I can never erase the shame that man brought on you and Papa!" he shouted. "I will see that he pays dearly," and he pounded the table with his fist.

Vito had changed his surname to Martino and had worked diligently achieving excellent references. After honorable employment as a majordomo he applied for such a position with Reno. He became indispensable to Reno who trusted him completely. As Reno's right hand man, he managed the estate, hiring and firing the servants and stable hands. He ordered the food and paid all the bills. Nothing that went on got by him. Yes, he would bide his time, he was a patient man. Vito would wait for the opportune moment to bring down havoc and disgrace upon Reno's reputation.

Martino had many partners in crime throughout Abruzzi

and beyond, even in Naples and Rome. Money was of no consequence, he had enough to carry out his dastardly plans. The following month these plans were set into motion. Elena's eighteenth birthday would be celebrated in early spring. Reno had been at his wits' end attempting to present her with the grandest gift he could think of. She had not conceived a child as yet, which in itself gave Reno great pain, thinking as he did that she was unhappy because she was barren.

Calling upon Martino for his advice, he found his majordomo very eager to help. "Your Highness, this gift must be one that will not only be a delight to receive, but also will give you great pleasure. Why not have a portrait painted by a famous artist! Perhaps an artist known in the Vatican!"

"By the good heavens, you have come up with the ideal gift, Martino," Reno cried out. "Yes, yes, the perfect gift." We must find the finest artist, Martino."

"I will do my very best, Your Highness. I have a very good friend in Rome; he knows artists who have painted beautiful portraits for the Vatican."

"I know you will give your complete attention to this matter," Reno remarked. "You know money is no object." He slapped Martino on the back.

"I will give it my complete attention, it will be my gift to Her Highness Elena," Martino spoke softly, bowing low. "We will place her portrait in the main hall for all to enjoy." The first phase of Vito's plan had been put in motion. Now, to complete his scheme.

Martino knew well Reno's desire to amass a fortune even greater than what he already possessed. He must whet the Count's appetite to pave the way with the implication of a secret diamond mine that Reno could not resist! That had to come first.

He strode quickly to his living quarters. Reno had given him the entire east wing of the castle. Bolting the door, he then opened a sliding panel that he had built himself. There were rows of files in alphabetical order any secretary would envy.

The files documented his association with the underworld, a task he had undertaken years ago. Schemes could be made and executed for any endeavor he wished to pursue, in this case, diamond mines, legal or illegal. Grabbing a tablet and pen, he wrote the name of someone to call and see in person. However, he knew he must pay bribes to underground friends so as not to get into trouble; these were treacherous men.

Before closing his files, he pulled out one marked 'artists.' The list was long of young men willing to go to any extent for a few thousand lire. I will look into this, Vito promised himself, after I talk with my contacts about the diamond mine. He rubbed his hands in anticipation and shouted to a vision of his father, "Papa! I will find a way to avenge you! We will have our vendetta!"

Martino was extremely busy the next few days contacting men of questionable trade, those possessing only the lowest means of survival. His pocket was full as he spoke with them, empty when finished, but Martino was satisfied he had obtained the correct information enabling him to go on with his plans. First, he would casually drop a few words to Reno.

"Your Highness, have you heard any reference to a secret diamond mine in Africa? This has come to may attention. Perhaps it is just an idle rumor," he said.

Reno sat up straight in his chair, greatly flustered and upset. "Why no," he said spilling his morning coffee.

"Your Highness, is every thing all right?" Martino inquired. "Is there anything I can do for you?"

"No, no, just call my carriage."

The trap was set.

Hurrying back to his quarters, Martino pulled out the file and slowly re-read it. After careful attention he found the penniless artist he sought and began making plans at once to meet with the unsuspecting culprit. Of course, Reno would have to meet the artist, Leo Palumbo, and give his permission. This had to be carefully undertaken, but Martino was eager to get things started.

Reno's mind was not on the artist and after giving the young man his indifferent handshake, announced he must leave on business and for Martino to take complete charge of the entire matter. Elena's portrait must be painted as soon as possible.

Martino gave his hand in compliance with Reno's approval. "I will make every effort to carry out your orders, Your Highness," he said with a smile.

Leo Palumbo's aristocratic features and blond good looks were inherited from his father, a wealthy nobleman with Danish ancestry. The child was the off-spring of one of his father's many mistresses. Early in life Leo showed an above average intelligence and a leaning toward artistic talent. His father managed a scholarship for his son to the prestigious Medici Accademia de Florence, where he spent two glorious years under the tutelage of some of Italy's finest artists.

When his scholarship ran its course, Leo went to Bartolemo and joined ranks with other struggling young artists, who had together rented a large studio. Here they lived and worked sharing their fortunes with one another. These were lean times and many nights their supply of food was inadequate. It was here that Leo was approached by Martino, who was certain he had found the ideal rogue in this desperate young man.

CHAPTER 10

Rosa made her new home at Castello del Sole with Contessa Juliana as her benefactress. Theirs had become a warm relationship with the Contessa regarding Rosa as the daughter she never had.

The Contessa and Elena did not share any activity at the castle unless invited. Reno's wing of the castle incorporated five complete accommodations. The two other sons, Pasquale and Guiseppe, remarked that one could house a complete army in Castello del Sole.

The weather had turned damp and Juliana was feeling pain in her limbs. Not one to complain, her discomfort was not discovered until Rosa saw Juliana rubbing her swollen legs. Rosa volunteered her help, and heating some olive oil, began to very gently massage Juliana's aching legs. Watching her keenly, Juliana was amazed that the pain was eased. Rosa had performed the same ritual for her mother who was constantly fatigued. Rosa's healing touch had brought warmth and comfort.

"If I had some eucalyptus leaves, I would boil them Your Highness. The oil is much more soothing and very fragrant."

"Do you know where we can get some of these leaves, Rosa?" Juliana asked, quite interested now.

"Yes, your Highness. Zio Matteo is due in a few days for his monthly visit. I will tell him where to gather the leaves," Rosa promised.

Matteo knew Rosa had healing powers and he did as he was bid. Rosa boiled the leaves, creating a pungent oil, which she applied to Juliana's body every evening at bedtime. Juliana could hardly believe the relief these ablutions brought her and she secretly blessed Rosa.

Because of the winter weather Rosa had not been back into the courtyard since her arrival and longed to sit in the lovely gazebo again. But she would not presume to be so bold and hoped the Contessa would invite her to sit there and read.

Every morning when she awakened she ran to her window hoping to see the sun. "When the day is sunny and warm again, it would be beneficial to sit outside and let the sun soak some warmth into your body, Your Highness," she suggested hopefully.

"Yes, Rosa, you are right. We shall wait for a sunny day."

But spring had not yet warmed the earth and she began to think the sun would never reappear. After weeks of dampness and fine mists, she was awakened by sunlight streaming through her window.

"This is the day I shall see the lovely courtyard," she thought excitedly and dressed hastily. Rosa was so excited at the prospect she did not secure her braids and, before they reached the outdoors, her long thick hair unfurled down her back.

Seeing her radiant face as they stepped into the flowered paths, Juliana thought there never had been anyone so beautiful. The Contessa's eyes were not the only pair to gaze on Rosa's lovely face that morning.

Paolo had been pruning his beloved roses when Juliana and Rosa seated themselves in the gazebo. Paolo was awe-struck at the sight of her. Had he had died and gone to heaven? Surely, this was an angel come to transport him to Paradise. Listening to her melodic voice, he dared not move for fear of breaking the spell. If I am dreaming I don't want to wake up, he thought.

Before long, Juliana, warmed by the sun and the sweet sound of Rosa's voice, relaxed completely and began to doze. Rosa stopped reading and began to gaze at the beauty around her. It was then she made contact with the blue eyes of a young giant. The equivalent of bells ringing, birds singing, and a delicious euphoria enveloped them both. Their eyes clung to each other and they were unaware of the world around them. Neither could look away.

Suddenly, Luigi appeared, loudly dropped his tools at Paolo's feet and broke the spell. None too soon, Luigi thought. He had observed the tableau before him, and becoming fearful of Paolo's absorption, stepped in. Juliana awakened with the loud noise and bade Rosa to follow her back into the castle.

Rosa and Paolo were never to be the same, each to dream of the other. Paulo had never seen real feminine beauty other than Elena. The beauty in his life had been the roses he tended with the love one would give a child. But this beautiful creature who entered his world that day was a distant dream that he longed to grasp and bring to reality. As he lay upon his cot that night, sleep would not come. When finally Paolo slept, he dreamed of a beautiful face framed with black curls falling down around it, and a voice that would live in his memory forever.

Rosa's heart beat wildly in her breast at the thought of the tall, handsome man in the courtyard. He had seemed to come out of nowhere, pulling her to him with the magnetism of his blue eyes. Had he stepped out of Homer's *Odyssey* as a magnificent Greek god? There was no sleep that night as she too quivered with excitement generated by that momentous encounter.

CHAPTER 11

*M*artino took great pains in his introduction of the artist Leo Palumbo to Contessa Elena de Salvatore, explaining his background as a student from the Medici Accademia. Elena was more impressed by his blond good looks and arrogant manner. Never having met any men of that ilk, she was eager to converse with him, but also surprised Reno would agree to approve of so young a man to be in her company alone. Little did she know her husband's mind was preoccupied elsewhere.

"Tell me, Signore Palumbo, what have you painted?"

"Landscapes, seascapes, portraits. I have the honor to paint your portrait, Your Highness."

"If you are to paint my portrait, please, call me Elena."

"Do you always get your own way?" he said laughing now. He was mocking her but she was fascinated by his smooth sounding voice.

Going over to Reno's liquor cabinet, he poured himself a glass of cognac. Poor little rich girl. All that money and she wants to play games. The poor bastard, the Count, is he really so stupid? His eyes wandered over Elena's young body, her golden hair and pale beauty. She is a beautiful woman, I could do worse and I need the money.

In the next few days work began on the portrait. As Leo's long, slender fingers guided his brush across the canvas, Elena was utterly fascinated and could not take her eyes away from him. Martino made certain Elena and the artist were not to be bothered and quietly set wine and canapes in the room, fresh cold fruit, and a splendid display of confections to entice them.

Leo looked around the huge room, "This place is like a museum, can't we find a more intimate spot to enjoy our repast?"

"Of course," Elena answered eagerly. She led him down a long hall and into her sitting room. Here she was in her element, surrounded by the soft draperies, shining crystal and delicate appointments.

Leo had made sure he brought with him several bottles of the wine Martino had so carefully laid out. Elena carried a small tray of the canapes and set it on her dresser.

Leo was very impressed with all the wealth and elegance displayed in minute detail. "This is a beautiful room, it suits you," he smiled as he opened a bottle of the wine. He then filled two glasses and presented one to her.

"We will drink to you and your beauty, Elena, and pray your portrait will do you justice," he whispered softly.

Elena had never consumed more than one or two glasses of wine at dinner time and she began to feel a warmth unknown to her. His voice was husky and hypnotizing as he leaned closer to her on the divan whispering erotic words in her ear.

Suddenly, Elena could hear her maid coming down the long hall and she moved clumsily away from him. Leo hastily hid the bottles of wine under the bed skirt of the king size bed.

"Yes," he said in a manner-of-fact voice, "I think we should choose the lighter color of blue for your gown in the portrait."

The maid entered the room and in an apologetic voice announced dinner would be ready in an hour. "Would Your Highness wish to dress for dinner?" she asked meekly.

"No, Serene, I think I shall lie down. Please see to it that Signore Palumbo has dinner in his room."

Elena slowly lay down on her bed and closed her eyes hoping her maid did not see her confused state. She needed a clear head, her whole body throbbed and she tried to catch her breath, which came in great gulps; her heart beat in painful movements. The tiny rosebud festooned to her gown rose and fell.

Rising, she stumbled to her vanity and reached for a wet towel bringing it to her hot temple. She ran to the sanctuary of her garden, trying to regain her composure. The cool air drifted over her and the cooing of doves calmed her feverish brow. She lay upon her lounge pallet until the rising moon came into her sight, then slowly made her way back to her room.

How can I face him on the morrow? She need not have wondered for when she entered the sitting room, he was there seated on the divan, drinking the last of the wine.

Slowly, he arose and crossed the room, and taking her face between his hands, kissed her first on her forehead, then tenderly on each cheek and the tip of her chin. "I waited for you my Princess," he whispered in a husky voice.

She slowly took out the hairpins holding her braided hair, letting the golden waves fall softly about her face and body. Her lips parted, waiting for his kiss, her heart pounding so hard she could feel it in her temples. But his lips traveled over her shoulders, and to the cleavage of her breasts. His hair brushed her lips, it was soft and smelled of musk. She ran her fingers through the blond curls of his head, pressing him ever closer to her. Then his hands were unbuttoning her bodice and he could feel the quiver of her body as he slid the gown over her hips. Finally, she stood naked before him, his eyes taking in her small, firm breasts and slender body. He picked her up and carried her to the bed. She lay with her arms outstretched waiting for the golden moment when his young, vibrant body would succumb to hers.

And so began a love affair between Leo and Elena. She fell madly in love with him, he was graceful and magnificently sexual. In Reno's absence, Leo lived at Castello del Sole in one of the unoccupied wings of the estate, only a few of the servants knew of his presence. Leo felt quite guilty having placed Elena in such a precarious situation. If Reno discovered their love affair, he could always escape to another part of Italy, but Elena would be left to suffer the consequences of their folly. The affair could only end in tragedy and Elena paced the floor night after night trying to find a solution to the frightening predicament she was in. She had believed she was truly barren and discovered she was pregnant. Leo was the father.

Prior to Reno's departure on a business trip, he was reminded that his mother would be celebrating her seventy years. "It will be a grand affair, Mama," Reno announced to Juliana. "I will contact Guiseppe and Pasquale and their wives, their children and some of the relatives that live in Bari, if you prefer."

"Oh, Reno, I would love to have Guiseppe and Pasquale and their wives and children, but no one else, just the family. I am too old for such excitement."

Guiseppe and Pasquale were pleased to do honor to their mother as all three men loved her. She had been kind and generous to the wives and their children.

Elena was not of the same mind, but reluctantly agreed to appear for the festivities. The party was a happy occasion, even Elena was impressed by Reno's endeavor to present her with a hastened party, as he had business to attend to.

Martino outdid himself and hired the finest chef in all of Abruzzi to create a grand display of exotic foods and wines that even the brothers and their wives had never seen before. As the drinking continued, the brothers became boisterous and jealous of Reno's grand display of wealth.

"You should not eat such rich foods!" Pasquale accused. "The real Roman men ate more fish and greens and they gave their strong wives children," he continued his tirade.

"You treat your wife like a piece of china. Be a man! Be a Roman! Thrust your spear like a real man!" Antonio shouted.

"Yes, our wives became pregnant on their wedding night," Guiseppe chimed in. Elena was aghast at such crude expressions and fled to her room. Reno was furious with his brothers and Elena's embarrassment. That night he took her to bed and fell upon her with such passion that it startled her.

Elena, in a frantic answer to her condition, suddenly remembered the tableau the two brothers had thrust upon her. "Yes, yes," she cried to herself. "That is the answer! I will tell Reno he had taken his brother's advice and became the Roman!"

CHAPTER 12

Elena had received only two brief letters from her husband. He had written that matters were progressing to his utmost satisfaction. He had offered a substantial portion of his silver and gold, the diamond mine would be worth much more, he reasoned. When he discovered he had been tricked, the mine was false, it was too late. He would not recoup his losses until many years later.

When Reno read Elena's letter telling him she was with child, he hurriedly packed his bags. "I am a father! I am a father!" he shouted to everyone he met on his travels back home. His losses set aside for now, his mind and heart were filled with joy. All he could think of was how he would create a majestic room for his unborn son. The nursery would be equipped with all the finest furniture, he even went so far in his mind's eye to think he would employ a nurse and governess to care for him.

When he arrived home he bestowed upon Elena so much jewelry and furs, she trembled at her deception; surely she would be punished somehow. The nuns always talked about God and His many promises to those who followed His golden rule. She was having nightmares so frightening that she could not sleep. Visions of herself reciting her catechism at the knee of her uncle, Archbishop Scolesi, rose up before her. His figure became the devil and he loomed over her and took the place of the devil, spitting fire in all directions.

Leo had come to say goodbye to Elena, a task he loathed to do. But he knew he could no longer stay at the castle. He had grown fond of Elena and regretted she was in love with him. He could see no solution but to leave and being somewhat cowardly, feared Reno's discovery of their clandestine affair. He would leave

Italy and emigrate to America. He did not tell Elena of his plans, it would have been too cruel. He told her he would go back to the commune until she gave birth and then she could send for him. They were not to communicate at all, difficult as that would be for her.

Elena was devastated and sobbed incoherently, she could not bear to be away from Leo so long. She knew it was wise for him to leave the castle and she promised to be brave. They would be together again soon. The portrait was finished and hung in the main hall creating an aura all its own. Leo had captured all of Elena's true beauty, from the golden hair that spilled over her shoulders to her translucent skin. But it was her eyes that sparkled with the joy of motherhood, or so it seemed to all.

Over the next months Reno fussed over Elena until she felt so suffocated that she screamed at him to leave her alone. He merely thought it was her condition that made her so irritable. He asked Juliana to look in on Elena in his absence, a task she took with good grace.

Juliana made a practice of visiting Elena several times a week as the young girl seemed to be in distress both mentally and physically, but she did not mention this to Reno. One day, while visiting Elena, she noticed Elena seemed to be very uncomfortable and kept rubbing her back in pain. "Elena, would you like Rosa, my companion, to massage your back? I know it will make you feel better, she has done a world of good for me."

"If you think it will help, please send her to me," Elena answered hesitantly. She had never had the comfort of a mother's love and was happy to have Juliana's sympathy. She was feeling poorly; she hated being pregnant and watched her growing body with alarm.

When summoned, Rosa brought not only the oil of eucalyptus but also a new oil she had concocted, a combination of chamomile and rose, it was soothing and relaxing with a more fragrant scent than the eucalyptus. As she stepped into Elena's sitting room she gasped in astonishment. Never had she seen a room so beautiful, the sight of the white harpsichord in the center of the lovely room filled her with awe.

"Come, Rosa," Juliana spoke softly, "I want you to meet my daughter-in-law, Contessa Elena." The two women, each of a different culture, were taken aback by the other's beauty. Elena, blue eyed, fair-skinned, with long golden hair, and Rosa, dark-eyed, olive-skinned, with ebony black hair that she wore in a magnificent crown on the top of her head.

Rosa curtsied, but Elena held out her hand in salutation. "I'm hearing wonderful things about you, Rosa. I do hope you can make this backache go away."

"Please come over to the bed, Your Highness, and lie down," smiled Rosa. "I will try to ease your pain."

Rosa drew Elena's gown to her waist and proceeded to massage her back with the fragrant oil. Elena sighed with contentment as Rosa's warm hands soothed her aching body, "Ah, Rosa, how good that feels," she whispered.

"I'm happy if it helps you, Your Highness."

Rosa had never seen such pale skin and marveled at the golden hair that spilled over her pillow. She massaged Elena's body until the young woman was asleep. Juliana covered her with a blanket and she and Rosa made their way back to their own quarters.

From then on, whenever Juliana visited Elena, Rosa was invited to go along. Elena learned Rosa read to Juliana ever day. She was surprised at Rosa's education being she had come from a poor family. Rosa explained she had been tutored by Padre Pietro and because of his growing concern for her, he had done an excellent job of giving her more than the basics of a good education.

Several weeks later, after the usual massage, she invited Rosa to inspect the roses and proceeded to tell her of Reno's discovery of the Rose Man. "His name is Paolo and he works magic with the roses. Come see, Rosa," and taking her hand, led her to where Paolo was working.

"Paolo, I want you to meet Rosa."

CHAPTER 13

*P*aolo and Rosa had not seen one another since their first encounter and seeing each other again was a happy occasion for both of them. Paolo shyly extended his hand in salutation after first wiping it on his worn pants. Rosa was trembling as she placed her small hand inside the large one offered her.

They stood there hands clasped, each not wanting to let go. After an embarrassing few seconds in which she reluctantly slipped her hand from his warm clasp, Rosa followed Elena through the masses of roses, exclaiming over each different species. Then turning to Paolo, she spoke to him for the first time.

"Thank you, Paolo, for showing me your roses."

Paolo smiled at her and, taking a pair of scissors from his pocket, cut off a ruby-red rose and handed it to her. He wanted to tell her that her beauty far surpassed the beauty of the rose, but did not know the proper words. Rosa's hand in his had been soft and warm, and as Paolo later told Luigi, felt like the petals from a rose.

Days later after the rose had lost its luster, Rosa pressed it and slept with it under her pillow. She longed to see Paolo again and her heart beat faster when she thought of his strong, warm hand holding hers. She had never had such strange feelings before and asked herself over and over, could this be what the poets call love?

Paolo had similar feelings of rare excitement beating in his chest and he too anticipated their next meeting. By questioning some of the maids he discovered Rosa was a companion to the Contessa Juliana and came from a poor family as he did. The only love he had known was familial love, but now he felt he was in love with this beautiful dark-eyed girl. Did he dare dream she felt as he did?

A week later, Elena sent word to Juliana for her permission to allow Rosa to join her in a discussion of a new book recently published. Rosa was overjoyed and set about braiding her thick black hair and pressing a clean gown. When she entered Elena's sitting room, her eyes rested on the white harpsichord. She had never seen the likes of such a piece and when Elena caught sight of the incredulous look on Rosa's face, she laughed loudly. Seating herself, she began to play the aria *Celeste Aida*, from Guiseppe Verdi's opera. When she finished she saw tears in Rosa's eyes.

"It is so beautiful, Your Highness, can you play more?" she asked timidly.

"Well, just one more. I want to ask your ideas on this new book," and with that played a lively tune.

"Come now, that's enough." Elena took Rosa's hand and led her to a love seat near an open window. Handing her a small book, she commanded her to read. The author, philosopher Bertrando Spaventa, was unknown to Rosa.

Rosa read the first chapter aloud in a shaken voice. Elena stopped her and said, "Well, what do you think of it so far?"

Rosa did not like the theme of the book as it was anti-Catholic and ugly in its interpretation of the Holy Scriptures; she told Elena so.

"Oh, Rosa, you are so saintly! Don't you ever question the teachings of the Church?" Elena spoke with such vehemence that Rosa was frightened.

Looking about her, she whispered fearfully. "Never! And you should not say such things or God may punish you. You must think of your unborn child."

Elena was indeed in need of prayer for the child she was carrying was not of Reno's seed. She had truly believed she was barren. When everyone supposed she was in her seventh month, she was actually nine months pregnant and extremely heavy with child.

Worriedly, Reno spoke to his physician, Doctor Felice.

According to the good doctor, she had two more months to full term, but she appeared to be in the final stages.

"It could be twins," Dr. Felice reassured Reno.

"God, I'll be relieved when this is all over," Reno sighed, wiping his brow. Elena had been in such a foul mood, he could not believe this screaming shrew could be his darling wife.

The weather had been sunny and warm all morning on the next day, with the golden sun lighting the courtyard and Paolo's roses spreading their aroma throughout the entire area.

Suddenly, a dark cloud appeared blocking the sun and a fierce wind began to howl, rain came in torrents, and trees bent over covering the lovely courtyard with broken limbs. The roses were in a shambles, their petals torn from their stems. Lightning shook the solid castle, and mud began to flow down the mountainside, covering the entrance.

Rosa went screaming into the large kitchen and into the terrifying arms of the cook, Josephina. They clung to one another crying.

Rosa could hear Elena screaming. The young girl ran to Elena's room. In her agony she cried out, "God forgive me!" The terrified woman lay upon her bed, covered with perspiration and tore at her gown in a frenzy. Talking to herself now she said over and over, "I must tell someone or I shall go mad." Rosa, that pillar of strength, I can tell her and get some relief from the terrible tension of carrying on this charade alone. She will never tell anyone.

The storm grew more intense, lightning bolts crashing to the ground. The two women, arms wrapped around one another, sobbed together, their tears mingling as one. Elena slowly began her confession to Rosa, every word bringing calm to the terrified woman. As she confessed quietly, even amidst Rosa's anguished murmurs, the storm abated and Elena was quiet. She went to her dresser, opened her drawer and brought out her rosary beads.

"Pray with me, Rosa, pray I will be forgiven. We can ask God to forgive me," she spoke softly. Rosa went down on her knees, the two of them reciting the familiar words they both had learned as children. When finished, Elena begged Rosa to stay with her. Rosa covered the spent young woman with a warm blanket and she lay down on the divan close enough to hear Elena if she was needed.

CHAPTER 14

*R*osa could not sleep, the confession she had heard was disturbing to her, and as she watched the sleeping Elena her heart ached for her, but she could not fathom how anyone who had such privilege and beauty could throw it all away.

Elena tossed and turned throughout the night throwing her blanket aside several times, crying out in her sleep. Rosa was awake and alert and covered the restless woman, afraid Elena should begin labor; she had no knowledge of the procedure needed.

Reno suddenly appeared at the door, his concern for his wife uppermost in his mind. When he saw Rosa tending his cherished wife, he began to shout at the helpless girl. "What are you doing, dirty peasant? Get out! Get out!" Reno screamed. "Get the doctor!" and stormed out.

Elena awakened, her nightgown soaking wet. She began to scream knowing she was in the first stages of her labor.

"Oh, Mother of God, she has broken her waters!" Rosa cried out. Not wanting to leave her alone, Rosa called for help. No one was about and since Rosa had never assisted at a birth, she attempted to get Elena undressed and into her bed.

But Elena in great pain and half out of her mind, stumbled toward the door, calling for the doctor. Rosa tried to restrain the terrified woman, who by this time had reached the steep stairway. In her agony, Elena lost her footing and fell the entire length of the stairs. By this time Rosa's screams were heard by her maid, Serene, who came running to the foot of the stairs where Elena lay in the final throes of birth.

Damien de Salvatore made his entry into the world at the expense of his mother, who lay dying on the marble floor. There had not been time to move her, and clasping Rosa's hand, Elena drew the girl's head down to hers and whispered, "Leo has a son, pray for my soul, Rosa."

Reno had been quickly summoned when he had gone to find the doctor. Upon reaching Elena's lifeless body, he screamed out in horror, "Who is responsible, what have they done to my beautiful flower!"

Sobbing loudly, he buried his face in her bosom. He was grief stricken and half crazy. Remembering Elena's last gesture to Rosa, he turned with such hatred, grasped her wrist and thundered at her in a voice that shook the poor girl so, it set her teeth to chattering. Rosa tried to speak but no words came.

"Tell me! Tell me what she said!" Reno was in an uncontrollable rage and in his misery, struck out at anyone. Unfortunately, it happened to be Rosa.

Hearing all the commotion, Paolo and Luigi had just reached the door leading from the courtyard when Reno struck Rosa across the face. Seeing Paolo, Rosa ran into his arms. Paolo's face was black with anger. Having witnessed this part of the terrible scene, he would have killed Reno with his bare hands, if it were not for Luigi and Rosa holding him back, entreating him to leave.

"Go! Get out! The three of you!" roared Reno with his fist raised in a sign of banishment.

The three ran to the gardener's shed where they stood with arms about one another. Rosa was still sobbing, not from the blow, but from the terror she felt over the devastating turn of events. Paolo held her close, stroking her hair and whispering softly all the while.

"It's all right, *piccina mia*, I will protect you."

Soon Rosa was quiet and the three of them sat in the little shed until darkness fell. They were startled by a soft knock on the door, and picking up a hoe in readiness for he knew not what, Paolo opened the door.

There stood a white-faced Juliana. She appeared to have aged considerably in the past few hours and Rosa gasped in anguish at the sight of her beloved mistress.

"Oh, Your Highness, how can we convey our deep sorrow?" Rosa cried.

"My sorrow is for you, child. My son should never have treated you so shamefully. I have come to tell you the Count has forbidden you, Paolo and Luigi to remain here. I cannot disobey him, therefore, I have to assist you in any way I can. I have a note for Padre Pietro that you shall deliver to him. The three of you can ride in the green grocer's cart back to your village. You will leave the first thing in the morning."

This was the longest speech Rosa had ever heard Juliana recite. Her heart was heavy at having to leave her mistress, but she was eager to escape the terror she felt.

"My crucifix! Rosa cried out. "I will not leave without it!"

"I have brought it along with your clothing and the broach I gave you," Juliana said softly handing to Rosa the beloved treasures wrapped in the shawl, along with a heavy envelope addressed to Padre Pietro.

Juliana sat with the three of them in the little shed until darkness fell. Whispering in Rosa's ear she said, "I found Elena's journal. I know the child is not Reno's, but until he realizes the tragedy, I will care for Damien. I need someone to love."

Relieved that someone else shared the bitter secret, Rosa said with great emotion, "I shall never forget you."

Then turning to Paolo, Juliana took his hand in both of hers, "Take good care of Rosa."

"Yes, Your Highness, I shall protect her with my life," Paolo promised earnestly.

"And goodbye to you Luigi," she said, nodding to the bewildered man.

Juliana was gone and Rosa never saw her again, but she would remember her all her life and benefit from her generosity.

CHAPTER 25

*P*aolo and Luigi bound up their belongings and Paolo made up a bed for Rosa. They slept in their clothes and at daybreak they climbed into the back of the grocer's cart and set out for Montelongo. Rosa knew the three of them could stay at her mother's home until they could find work.

The ride was long and bumpy, the grocer stopping for a short while so they could relieve themselves. Luigi had brought along some apples and cheese he had received from the cook, Josephina, for their long trip. They arrived in the village at dusk and headed for Rosa's home.

But to Rosa's bewilderment, a strange man came to the door as she entered. She did not like the looks of him, he was unkempt and smelled of wine.

"Where is my mother?" Rosa asked as he barred the door.

"And who is this fine lady?" he leered at her.

Not answering, Rosa called out, "Mama, where are you?" A woman heavy with child came into the room where Rosa, Paolo and Luigi stood. Rosa sucked in her breath, this sad looking creature was indeed Maria.

"Mama, who is this man and how could you be with child?"

The strange man turned on her with a boozy smile and said, "So, this is our little benefactress. Well, come and give your new Papa a kiss."

"Stay away from me. Mama, tell me it's not true! Why wasn't I told?" Rosa spoke with disbelief.

Paolo stepped to her side in a movement that made the man retreat in fear.

Taking Rosa aside Maria spoke with difficulty. "Carlo is my

new husband." She tried to explain. "For the first time in my life there was no man in the house. In spite of Antonio's weaknesses, I at least had some one to share my misery."

She had met Carlo at a neighbor's wedding and was flattered by his attention. Little did she know he had heard she received large amounts of money from a wealthy Contessa. She did not heed the warnings of her friends that Carlo had no job and was only after the income from Rosa. It felt good to have a man pursue her and it was not long after the initial meeting that they were married. Bitterly, she realized his true intentions when it was too late and now she was saddled with another drunkard.

"I still don't know how you could marry someone like him," Rosa accused.

Saying nothing to her remark, Maria spoke sharply to Rosa, "Why are you here and not at the castle? Who are these men?"

"We no longer live or work at the castle. Mama. I will tell you the whole story. We want to stay here until Paolo and Luigi can find work. They are my friends."

Carlo shouted, "What do you mean you don't work at the castle any more? What about the monthly stipend?"

"We have no money," Rosa replied.

"No money? No money?" Carlo repeated. His meal ticket was in jeopardy. "Well, now Rosa," he began in a much sweeter tone. "You can get work here in the village and give your wages to your Mama as before."

"Whatever money I make I will keep now that Mama has an able-bodied man to look after her," Rosa retorted.

"No money, no room!" Carlo exclaimed, shaking his fist at Rosa and the two men who had stood by silently. He left the house in a rage and Rosa looked at her mother sadly, glancing at the condition of her former home, which was in worse condition than when she left.

Paolo spoke up, "Come, Rosa. We will leave this place. The Contessa gave us instructions to see Padre Pietro and that is what we are going to do." He had spoken in a soft yet commanding voice and Rosa followed him out the door.

Looking back at her mother, she felt she was looking at a stranger. Mama never sent word she had remarried. She took my wages and gave them to that awful man. Tears filled her eyes as she remembered the once beautiful Maria holding hands with her handsome Antonio, laughing up into his eyes. She pictured a day at the seashore many years ago, the three of them running along the beach holding hands. There had been good days before her father's accident.

Rosa would never see or hear from her mother or her brothers and sisters again. Zio Matteo Totto had not returned from his last journey and no one knew where the poor soul was. Rosa could only wonder and pray for all of them.

CHAPTER 16

*D*id Vito Martino have his vendetta? Elena was dead, she was beyond hurt. Leo had left Italy and was living somewhere in America. The other servants lived in fear for their jobs and cloaked themselves in *omerta*, the protective silence of complicity; they were not about to reveal anything. The future brought a changed Reno. He began to share what remained of his wealth with his brothers, trying to make amends for all his past transgressions.

Although Reno de Salvatore had been nearly ruined by Martino's duplicity, he had recovered much of his lost fortune, for he too had criminal friends whom he paid handsomely to help raise him out of debt. Vito should have enjoyed knowing that Reno would never recover from the grief of losing Elena, a much worse fate than losing his wealth. But Vito believed he had failed to avenge his father and felt himself in disgrace. He set out for parts unknown taking his aged mother with him.

In his grief, Reno barely looked at the child. He saw the pale skin and blue eyes of Elena and hated the infant for causing her death. He begged Juliana to care for the baby in fear God would punish him for his aching heart, that in spite of his wealth, it had only brought him a sorrow from which he could never recover.

Fearing his own mortality, the Count made provisions in his will to provide for his brothers, Pasquale and Guiseppe, as well as mother, Juliana, and his son, Damien. Should anything happen to him, he demanded a portion of his wealth be divided among those families he had left destitute years before. Perhaps, in this manner, he could make amends to God, and escape the eternal fires of hell.

Juliana guarded the newborn infant so carefully none but his nurse was able to glimpse him. She was his *nonna* (grandmother) and would never speak of the circumstances of his birth to anyone. She showered him in affection and attention with all her being, trying to replace a mother's love.

As fate would have it, just months after executing his Last Will and Testament, Reno was killed while riding one of his gigantic steeds in the wild mountains of Montelongo. Both he and the animal plummeted over a cliff to their immediate deaths.

In the years that followed, Castello del Sole would be sold at auction to a wealthy American, the owner insisting the portrait of Elena remain in the entrance hall for his friends to admire. When Pasquale took control of the castle after the American failed to make payment, he immediately removed the painting.

The lawyers handling the estate were directed to establish a park on the grounds where children would happily play. A statue of Count Reno de Salvatore was erected as benefactor and the park was dedicated to his beloved Elena. Despite Pasquale's protest, it would now be known as Parco di Elena, in perpetuity.

CHAPTER 17

*R*osa led the way to St. Anthony Church where she had so many childhood memories. Padre Pietro had tutored her on Saturdays, lending her books he had received from Friar Phillipe Bellini at the Franciscan Mission in Campobasso. He was so proud of her as an eager pupil.

Padre struggled to demonstrate to the other children that if they followed her example, they too, could become good students, but it was lost upon them. Their parents had no desire to aid them in becoming good students, they were needed to work with their fathers. Rosa tried to encourage them also, but her words were lost. She attempted to make the good priest feel his words were helping her in her quest to seek knowledge.

Seeing Rosa, Padre Pietro opened his arms wide and embraced her. "Oh, Rosa, my child. It is so good to see you! And what are you doing here?" he cried out with deep emotion.

"Padre, why wasn't I told about my mother and that awful man?" Rosa queried, giving the priest a puzzled look.

"We thought your life was so much better at the castle, Rosa. You had an opportunity to better yourself and live in a fine home. Please understand," he begged.

"I understand your good intentions, Padre," she replied with much sadness in her voice. And with that, she handed the envelope Juliana had sent him. Before he opened the envelope they recounted all that had happened. Paolo did most of the talking, which pleased Rosa. He went through all the events, clearly much to Luigi's surprise.

"Tsk, tsk, how terrible! And what a tragic end for the young wife and mother, may she rest in peace." He murmured sympathetically, "And the young child?"

"Contessa Juliana has promised to care for him," Rosa answered.

Padre Pietro nodded. "Now, if you will excuse me," he said. "The envelope says personal and confidential. I will retire to my study."

The three sat in the chapel, Rosa was crying. "I love her so much," Paolo thought. "I would gladly die for her; I want to love and protect her always." He was only a peasant but his thoughts were that of a nobleman.

Luigi watched the two of them and saw the sweet face of Rosa praying and Paolo gazing at her in adoration. What's to become of these two, he worried. How can an old man like me be anything but a burden. God help us!

An hour later the priest came out. Motioning them into his study, he bade them to be seated. "You may sleep in the church tonight using the pews for beds. I have written a letter to Friar Phillippe at the mission. He will give you shelter until you can find work."

"Padre," Paolo whispered, "I would like you to marry Rosa and me. That is if she will have me," he added, looking shyly at Rosa. Then, getting up, he went over to where Rosa sat. Taking her hand, he knelt beside her and said, "Rosa, will you marry me?"

In a voice choked with emotion, Rosa replied softly, "Yes, Paolo."

"And I will give the bride away," Luigi said gleefully, as he danced a little jig.

"Very well, Paolo, I will preform the ceremony tomorrow at dawn, and then you can be on your way. It will take all day to reach Campobasso, so you had better bed down for the night. I will give you some blankets."

Turning to Rosa he said in a low voice, "Rosa, I am so happy for you. You have worked hard all your young life. You have learned so much at my knee and I am proud to send you to Friar Phillippe at the mission. You have found a good man for a husband, I know he will care for you."

It was an emotional time for the priest. He had baptized Rosa as an infant and helped her study catechism to make her First Communion. He had assisted at her Confirmation and now he would join her in Holy Matrimony with one he judged to be a kind and good man.

They made their beds on the pews and Paolo leaned over Rosa, placing a blanket over her slender body. Then he leaned down and kissed her softly on the lips. Rosa reached up and returned his kiss.

Paolo arose before the sun's rising. Rosa was sleeping quietly and Luigi was snoring noisily at the back of the chapel. Paolo remembered on their journey the previous day they had passed a field of wild poppies. Hurrying, he made his way to the field and picked a huge armful of the bright, red flowers. Returning, he stood beside the pew where Rosa slept.

Just then, Rosa opened her eyes and her first glance fell on Paolo, his arms loaded with the bright poppies.

"They are for your bridal bouquet, I wish I could give you more," he murmured.

"Oh, Paolo, they are so beautiful," she whispered with tears in her eyes.

She went to the well in the courtyard and washed her face. Then gathering the poppies in her arms, she said in a happy voice, "Today is my wedding day! My heart is filled to the brim!"

The dreams she had held in her heart were coming true; she ached with love for this man standing beside her. She did not see the poor clothing or the worn boots, there was only the brilliance of his smile and the warmth of his eyes.

They were married in a simple ceremony. Luigi held Rosa's hand and then placed it in Paolo's. Tears rolled down the old man's wrinkled face.

The long trek to Campobasso took all day as there was no need to hurry. They carried another heavy envelope addressed to Friar Phillipe Bellini at the Franciscan Mission. They arrived at nightfall, weary, but filled with great expectation.

The Friar greeted them warmly and invited them into the quiet, old mission. Paolo introduced himself, Rosa and Luigi, gave Friar Bellini the envelope, and explained the reason for being there. "Come, come, my children, you are welcome to share some bread and cheese with us," the Friar said jovially.

Leading them to the huge kitchen, he bade them sit down on one of the long planks. He brought out a loaf of dark bread, cut off a generous piece of cheese from a large, yellow wheel, and laid out three glasses. Almost tenderly, he opened a bottle of rich, red wine and told them to help themselves.

They ate hungrily thanking the kind Friar. Luigi was astonished the good man would offer them wine of such quality and commented on it. Pleased, Friar Bellini said he would show them his grape vines in the morning, explaining they made their own wine.

After they had eaten, Paolo carefully withdrew the marriage certificate from his knapsack and explained to the Friar, "We were married this morning by Padre Pietro."

"My blessings on you both and may you have many children," he smiled, making the sign of the cross over their heads. He then arose, and taking three candles, led them to the upper stairway. He gave them each a candle and showed them to their rooms.

"I know you are tired after your long journey," the Friar sympathized. Rest well and we will talk in the morning."

Paolo and Rosa were finally alone. The room contained a bed and a small wooden chest of drawers. A pine table with a lavebo stood in one corner, a tiny window overlooked the valley below.

They gazed at one another, not speaking. The room was suddenly beautiful as love shone in every corner. Paolo drew Rosa to the bed and, sitting beside her, began to undo her long braids.

Black curls spilled to her waist. Slowly, Rosa unbuttoned her dusty gown and then, even more slowly, removed the rest of her garments until she stood before him more beautiful than a marble statue. The moon shone through the open window bathing her body in a silvery glow. Paolo burned with desire, but did not want this glorious moment to end. He stood before her in his splendid, naked manhood. Caressing her body he spoke huskily, "I have never been with a woman before, Rosa."

She replied softly, "I have never been with a man."

Their union was sweet and passionate, each awakening to joy never experienced before. Their bodies cried out for one another and it was not until almost dawn that they fell asleep in one another's arms.

The next morning after breakfast, the Friar led them outdoors behind the mission and there before them, was the magnificent valley completely covered with grape vines; they gasped at the sight. Friar Bellini extolled the abundance of their annual crop explaining the success of the winery. Next came a tour of the giant casks fermenting into the robust wine they had drunk the night before.

Then, ordering them to accompany him to his study, he invited them to be seated. Opening the envelope they had delivered from Padre Pietro, Friar Bellini read the enclosed letter.

My dear friends:

Each of our lives is filled with joy and sorrow. We must relish the joy and hold it in our hearts as a refuge for the bitter sorrows, which will befall us all. We must learn from every experience and go on unafraid.

I have instructed the good Friar to assist you in booking passage to America. Your passage has been paid and I have provided enough savings to see you through for a short while. I have enclosed the address of my son, Carmine de Salvatore, who immigrated to America in 1860 and who now works and resides in the Ohio Valley. I have instructed him to assist you in any way he can. Go with God and remember me in your prayers.

Respectfully,

Contessa Juliana de Salvatore

At the close of the letter, silence fell in the room, broken only by Rosa's quiet weeping. Their happiness at this unexpected and joyous turn of events held them in a euphoric state and they embraced and kissed one another repeatedly.

The time of their departure for the great ship to carry them to America was not for six weeks. During this time Rosa learned Friar Bellini spoke five languages, one of which was English. At her insistence, he tutored her in the spoken English word while she eagerly studied a slim volume containing the basics of the English language that the kind Friar had given her.

"So, at last I meet the little lady who made Padre Pietro beg books from me," smiled the Friar.

"Yes," she laughed, her eyes shining in their eagerness. "I want to learn all I can. I have always loved books. Now I can learn to speak well enough when we arrive in America."

Friar Bellini was amazed at her determination and the way she retained every word. She worked late into the night, writing and then pronouncing each sentence over and over. She spoke only English to him, however incorrect until he corrected her. Then she repeated the proper words in a suitable fashion.

During all this time, Paolo and Luigi had made themselves useful. They rebuilt parts of the crumbling stone wall surrounding the mission. When that was completed, Paolo cultivated a large plot of land on which Luigi planted corn from seeds the Friar had given him.

"Ah, Paolo and Luigi" the Friar said as he surveyed their

handiwork. "You have more than paid for your keep here. I am going to miss you."

Each night Paolo and Rosa delighted in their loving relationship, finding great joy in one another. "I never knew life could be so beautiful," whispered Paolo as he wrapped his arms about Rosa.

"I love you so, Paolo my dearest." She answered, snuggling against his warm, naked body. "Take me to your heart," she implored with tears in her eyes. "Never let me go."

"Never," he whispered, his lips against her hair.

Their coming together was the culmination of a haunting desire and longing that affected both their lives. It was as though a light had exploded within them and its radiance enveloped their very souls. They basked in its warm glow.

Meanwhile, there was a problem of obtaining a wardrobe for the three of them. Rosa still had the clothing Contessa Juliana had given her but lacked a warm coat, and Paolo and Luigi had only the clothes on their backs. Friar Bellini rummaged through the boxes of clothing he collected for the poor and found several suitable changes of trousers for the two.

Finding a shirt for Paolo was a problem due to the size of his chest. The patient Friar went begging in the village and returned triumphant carrying with him two shirts and a black wool jacket for Paolo as well as a coat for Rosa. Paolo had never owned so many garments and when the Friar turned them over to him, tears welled up in his eyes. Luigi was able to be fitted from the boxes at the mission. They were now ready for their long journey.

The night before their departure, Rosa knelt at the mission altar reflecting on the unexpected and happy events that had taken place in the last six months. She and Paolo would raise a family in America and become citizens of that glorious country. The doorway to her new life was opening up and her heart was filled with joy and gratitude.

Part Two:

AMERICA

Chapter 28

The steamship, SS Idaho, with two masts rigged for sail, groaned and creaked out of the Port of Napoli on a stormy day in September 1870 into rough seas. In the next ten years, 55,000 Italians would come to the United States. In the 1880s, they numbered 300,000; in the 1890s, 600,000; in the decade after that, more than two million. People who could not afford anything better were crammed into every corner of steerage class, in reality the cargo hold, and the stench of perspiring bodies permeated the air.

But the dream of a life in America filled with freedom in every sense of the word, along with the promise of gold in the streets just for the taking, gave them a fortitude to endure any adversity. They were an ethnic mix and the babble of foreign tongues rang throughout. The three travelers were happy to be among such an enthusiastic crowd, all in an eager state of mind, looking forward to a new home and life, their dreams coming true.

The first few days the sea was calm and there was singing and happy laughter. One man had brought a cherished concertina and several others had harmonicas which made a lively combination. Even though there was a difference in the spoken language, all knew the language of song, and there was a loud clapping and stomping of feet.

On the fourth day, the ship began to heave and toss in the stormy weather, and the laughter and singing ceased. Many could not hold food on their stomachs. Children cried through the night, while mothers, sick themselves, tried to comfort them. The wooden bunks were small with no mattress to ease an aching, tired body.

Rosa had become ill and Paolo feared for her health. She seemed to grow thinner every day until Paolo in desperation tried vainly to entreat the ship's mate to allow him to carry her out into the cold, clear air. On their departure, Friar Bellini had given Rosa his English language book, which on the first calm days she had studied. In her halting English she attemped to convey what Paolo was saying in sign language.

Seaman Sean O'Flaherty was a father of six sons and four daughters, along with being a religious man, so when he looked upon Rosa's wan face, he exclaimed, "Holy Mother of God! That wee thing will niver make it to shore. If the Cap'n catches me helping thim folks, it'll be the divil to pay!"

But suddenly, Sean caught sight of Rosa's crucifix, which she had clutched to her breast. "Sure now, are ye Catholic?"

When Rosa heard that word, she nodded her head vigorously and kissed her crucifix.

"Well, now, as one Catholic to another, sure we got to stick together."

In all good conscience, he knew he had to help them and with that he took out some blankets and quietly pushed them out the door. On deck he found a sheltered spot and, motioning them to be quiet, went about his duties.

Paolo wrapped Rosa in the warm blankets and sat holding her close. Raising her pale face, Rosa reached up and kissed him lightly. Looking at the dark circles under her eyes, he suddenly remembered the lovely girl of his dream. Rosa! Thoughts raced frantically through his mind. If I lose Rosa I have nothing to live for, no family, very little money, and on the way to a strange land. From deep in the almost-forgotten recesses of his memory, he hummed a lullaby his mother had sung to him as a little boy.

"Paolo, we will be a real family, soon," Rosa said softly.

"A real family?" Paolo asked in bewilderment.

"Yes, dearheart, I'm carrying our child," Rosa answered, her face buried against his chest.

Holding her even closer, Paolo began to pray earnestly, asking God to help her. The sea calmed and Rosa began to rally when Sean brought her some tidbits from his evening meal.

"She's like my own wee one," he tried to explain to Paolo, taking out a creased photo.

Paolo pointed to Rosa's stomach indicating her pregnancy.

"If that don't beat all, now," shouted Sean, pumping Paolo's hand.

Paolo and Rosa exclaimed over the lovely child's face in the photo.

"Don't ye worry a bit, folks, old Sean will take care of ye," the good man exclaimed.

Care for them he did, bringing a pillow from his own bunk for Rosa's comfort. Skipping a meal now and then, he was able to provide Rosa with adequate good food and drink. Paolo was profuse in his thanks to Sean, but the mate waved away any gratitude by saying, "I pray God will reward my children for what I do for others."

After the 18-day voyage, Sean said, "I've come to tell ye we'll be putting into the harbor soon and ye can see the Lady With The Lamp. Aye, and 'tis a sight ye will remember all yer life."

All passengers were allowed on deck for the glorious moment when that towering edifice came into sight at the gateway to their new world, holding her lamp high, the very symbol of freedom. Men and women wept, young boys cheered, and the ship's whistle added to an overwhelming and joyous bedlam.

"America! America! Was the jubilant cry as the ship came into the harbor.

Why did they come? The most powerful reason for most immigrants during the mid-1800's was hard times in the homeland. The poor in Europe chose America because they had heard that all the old orders had been thrown out with the American Revolution. They came to believe that life in America, in any condition, would be better than at home.

Word spread throughout southern and central Europe that a decent life lay ahead where one could work, practice religious freedom, enjoy civil liberty, and provide their children with abundant food and schooling. They had never heard of George Washington or Thomas Jefferson, but photographs were sent back to the old country of well-fed families, of a father or cousin wearing new shoes or suit as a doctor or merchant would.

In the remote villages of the Abruzzi, such as Rosa's village, Montelongo, politics were closely followed by people who had never been to America and who could neither read nor write. "The Roosians are bringing their own wheat to America," they exclaimed. "They are planting it by the ton."

"They are a tough bunch, them Roosians," cried another.

The Homestead Act of 1862 granted 160 acres of free land to claimants who would work the land and produce a crop in five years, allowing nearly any man or woman a chance to live the American dream. America was looked upon as the country destined to lead the world in a new age of prosperity, liberty and human progress. In the 1870's, there were more immigrants coming into the United States from Italy than any other country.

The ship was now in the harbor and the immigration inspectors boarded from a cutter which had come alongside. The Captain was required to note on the ship's manifest cases of yellow fever and leprosy. The unlucky ones were taken in a quarantine boat to a special island and deported as soon as possible. Eventually, the engines began to hum again and there ahead of them was the Manhattan horizon, a true sight to behold. The newcomers sorted out their bundles on the dock amidst a babble of languages, and then all were tagged with numbers. They were cleared for entry at Castle Garden.

They were crowded into a main building where they heard immigration officers hollering out numbers in Italian, German, Polish, Russian, Hungarian and Yiddish. According to their numbers, they were led down corridors where a doctor in a blue uniform officiated. He was a tough diagnostician who examined them from head to foot. Little children, held by their mothers, had to step down to see if they had rickets.

After the physical ordeal, they were asked countless questions: Who paid their passage? How many dependents did they have? Were they ever in prison? Were they an anarchist? Was there a job waiting for them? When all questions were answered satisfactorily, they were given a landing card and taken to a currency booth to change lire, or whatever, into American dollars. From there they were sent to a travel agent or "railroad man" who was familiar with the city streets.

Rosa presented to the railroad man the de Salvatore address, which Juliana had given them. After haggling over the cost of tickets, they were on they way, riding through open countryside with Cleveland, Ohio their destination.

Rosa held tightly to Paolo's arm. "Suppose they had sent us back, Paolo?" she said, badly shaken by their landing and especially the memory of her physical examination. Paolo had been extremely nervous with the entire procedure, especially being separated from Rosa, and when they met in the lobby afterward, he was greatly relieved.

The train ride from New York to Cleveland was approximately five hundred miles. It was their first look at America. Luigi gazed in wonder at the rolling hills, manicured farms and the crystal clear Lake Erie, the Ohio and Cuyahoga Rivers. Paolo and Rosa sat, hands locked together, staring at the sturdy homes with children laughing and playing in green meadows, women hanging clothes over lines strung across back yards.

Mile after mile of wheat and cornfields rustled softly in the autumn breezes. A barefoot boy, fishing pole slung over his shoulder and a mess of fish dangling from a rope, held up his catch in salutation and waved, grinning, as they went by. Instinctively, Rosa waved back and turning to Paolo, exclaimed, "Oh, Paolo, did you see? That will be our son in a few years."

"Yes, little one, and he will be healthy and strong," Paolo answered, smiling.

"And free," Luigi interrupted.

"You were free Luigi," Rosa said in surprise. "Why do you say that?"

"No, Rosa, I wasn't free. I worked all my life for a master who never knew me. He gave me nothing and took all my strength for a few pennies a day. I spoke with some of the men aboard ship who have sons and cousins that came to America years ago and already have their own homes with money in the bank. No one tells them where to go and they answer to no one. If they plant wheat or corn they plant it and it belongs to them to sell at market or to keep for their family."

"They tell great stories, Luigi," returned Rosa. "Each time its told the story grows bigger and better. We shall wait and see."

Then taking out her English book she began to study pronouncing each word according to the idiomatic phrasing. Paolo watched her tenderly, smiling all the while at the determination she expressed going over each word many times.

"Paolo, we must learn English together. We cannot disappoint Contessa Juliana by our ignorance. My name in English is Rose, you are Paul, and Luigi is Louis."

"Hey! No Louis! I'm Luigi! Don't fool around with my name!" hollered the old man. "I've been Luigi Romano all my life and nobody changes that!"

"Rosa didn't mean to offend you, Luigi. She is only trying to help us to become Americans."

"I don't want to be American! I'm proud of being Italian. I only want a decent life in a free country and I will never be anything but Italian until I die!" he answered emotionally. And with that got up from his seat next to Paolo and Rosa and sat alone at the end of the train looking out the window disconsolately.

"I think he is afraid, Rosa" Paolo said.

"Yes, I thought that when we boarded the train. I will apologize. He is a dear old man, and I love him as you do, Paolo," Rosa answered thoughtfully. "But you and I must learn if we are to find work."

"You will not work, Rosa, not with the baby on the way," Paolo said with determination. "I will work for both of us."

Rosa was not quite sure she agreed, but having offended Luigi did not want to also offend Paolo by her independent manner. She had always worked and felt that laziness was one of the worst habits one could acquire. But she said nothing and went back to her studying.

They rode all day and when darkness fell, Rosa curled up next to Paolo and slept. But Paolo could not sleep. Everything seemed to be happening so fast. How could he tell Rosa that he too was filled with fear? Fear of the unknown, how to provide for a wife and coming child, and would the de Salvatores greet them with warmth, or contrary to Rosa's dream, with cold indifference?

The next day as they neared Cleveland, the scenery changed dramatically. The Cuyahoga River was lined with sawmills, coal docks, blast furnaces, and over all hung black smoke. Oil tanks rose up like forts and at times the oil glaze on the river caught fire. Schooners and steamers crowded the river mouth, here were elevators, mills and furnaces.

The three travelers were dismayed with these sights. Had they left sunny Italy with its pristine skies for this terrible stench and smoke-filled air? They looked at one another sadly, each not wanting to put into words their bitter disappointment.

Chapter 19

It was late afternoon when the train pulled into the Cleveland depot. Gathering up the wicker basket that contained their few possessions, the three alighted and went into the large train station. The station was like a thriving metropolis, people hurrying to and fro, women with small children in tow, business men carrying bulging briefcases and through it all pervaded the aroma of fresh roasted peanuts and popcorn mingled with brewed coffee.

The three hungry travelers could not resist the smell of fresh coffee and for a penny each, obtained three huge mugs of the delicious brew. Having emptied their mugs to the last drop, Rosa again presented the address to the station master and asked directions as best she could with her limited vocabulary.

The station master looked them over from head to toe, saw their shabby clothing and the wicker basket, and shaking his head in disbelief said, "Euclid Avenue? There must be some mistake. That street is only for swells, what could you be doing at such a place?"

"But it's right," insisted Rosa.

"Well, must be you are the new servants. They are scraping the bottom of the barrel these days," returned the station master with great disdain.

Rosa did not understand this comment and kept pointing to the address.

"Take the Euclid Avenue street car down the street," he motioned toward the southern exit. "Get off at the end of the line." He turned and strode away muttering under his breath, "Damn greasy Ayetalians."

The three waited at the exit until Rosa spotted the huge letters, EUCLID, on the street car banner and jumping aboard sat in the front seats. "How far are you going?" asked the surprised conductor.

Rosa showed him the address and he answered very brusquely, "That will be three cents."

So far their day had cost them 12 cents and Paolo leaned over to Rosa "We must be very careful with the money, Rosa," he said anxiously,

"Yes, Paolo, I know. Once we get there we will be alright," answered Rosa.

As the street car left the dirty city limits and progressed along Euclid Avenue, they saw quite a different picture. Here was a regal street lined with mansions and gardens, English manor houses, French chateaux, Italian villas, and palazzos graced the avenue. Its opulence dazzled and the three of them became extremely excited.

"You see, Paolo, its like being at the castle again. We will have work here as the Contessa promised," cried Rosa joyfully.

Upon arriving at the end of the line, the conductor turned and spoke to them, "This is as far as we go, folks. You walk the rest of the way."

"But how far?" questioned Rosa

"About a mile straight down the road. You'll see the numbers on the mail box," and with that headed back for the city.

They stood in the middle of the street. Rosa caught the word "mile" and the conductor had pointed in the southern direction.

"I think we go down this street for a mile, Paolo," she explained.

Paolo smiled good-naturedly, "Well, Rosa, a mile isn't too far, and it's a beautiful day." He wished he could understand this new language.

He and Luigi carried the wicker basket between them and they walked in the direction the conductor had given them.

Occasionally, a fine carriage passed, the occupants casting cold stares at the shabby trio. Soon, Rosa spotted the numbers 402 on a mailbox. "This is it! This is it!" she cried.

Before them stood a magnificent pink Italian villa, with a huge stone fountain enhancing the courtyard. Meekly, they went to the front door, but it appeared so imposing they hurriedly walked to the rear of the building. Knocking on the door, their hearts filled with trepidation, they waited. Suddenly, the door opened and a huge man, resplendent in uniform, stood in the doorway scowling down at them.

"Well, what do you want?" growled the imposing figure.

"Please, sir. We are looking for Signore Carmine de Salvatore," said Rosa in a shaky voice.

"He is not here," snarled the uniform.

'When will he return?" Rosa insisted.

"He is out of the country and will not return for a month," he snapped and slammed the door shut.

So startled were they that no one spoke. Tears came to Rosa's eyes and suddenly her body was overcome with weariness.

"He is not here and he won't be back for a month, I think," she replied with a quavering voice.

Paolo's worst fears had come true. What to do? In their naïveté they had come thousands of miles in pursuit of a promise. Their only error a belief that, against all odds, fate would deal with them kindly.

The two men stared at one another, neither able to grasp the reality of their situation. Paolo held Rosa in his arms trying to comfort her when suddenly, a wizened old man, half hidden by the shrubs surrounding the rear entrance, jumped out and whispered in Italian, "Hey, paisani, come with me."

The three were so surprised to see the odd creature, but most of all to hear someone speaking in their native tongue, that they hurriedly followed the old man into a grand stable behind the villa.

"Who are you and can you help us?" quickly asked Paolo.

"My name is Rocco Valenti and I am the keeper of the stable. I heard you asking for Signore de Salvatore and that low-down butler, Alberto, telling you lies. But tell me who you are and what are you doing here? Looks like you just got off the boat," said the old man, giving them a quizzical look.

"We are so happy to see one of our countrymen, Rocco," Paolo said with great relief. They related all that had happened to them in the past few months, leaving out only the part about the money they carried. It was best not to disclose their financial status before a perfect stranger. They learned Rocco had arrived from Salerno five years before and had worked for the de Salvatores for the past three years.

"He's a son of a bitch, pays peasant wages and makes me work 14 hours a day." As he recounted he spat tobacco juice on the ground in a large arc.

"Is he out of the country as that terrible man said?" asked Rosa.

"Out of the city probably. He has a mistress in Youngstown. He could be gone for a week or so. Do you have family here?" asked Rocco.

"No, we have no one. Can you tell us where we can stay until I can find some work?" asked Paolo in a worried voice.

"Well, I have a *comare* (godmother) who has a rooming house in the city. She rents a room for 50 cents a week and for another 20 cents she gives you a bowl of soup every day," Rocco told them. "Tomorrow is Sunday and I have to go into the city to see my sons. I will take you there. Tonight you can stay in the stable, no one will know you are there."

Relieved at their good luck, the three settled down for the night in the warm stable. Paolo was wary however, and slept lightly listening for every sound. Glancing up, he saw a large piece of timber lying across one of the stalls. Picking it up he felt safer with some sort of weapon on hand.

Dawn came and soon they were walking back to the city with Rocco as their guide. He brought them to a huge, old house in a dirty part of the city. Rosa was dismayed when she saw the rundown neighborhood and held tightly to Paolo's arm.

Seeing her discomfort, Paolo leaned down and whispered in her ear, "We will stay here only until I find work, I promise, Rosa, I promise."

Much to her relief, Rocco's *comare*, by name of Felicia, was plump and jovial and hugged Rosa to her voluptuous breast. Her white hair was tightly pinned back in a bun at the nape of her neck. Her apron was voluminous and clean, Rosa noted. A tantalizing aroma greeted them as they stepped inside a bright, clean kitchen and when Rocco explained their plight, Felicia hollered out, "Come, come, sit down and have a nice bowl of minestrone!"

The food was like nectar of the gods and they ate ravenously. Rosa insisted on cleaning up the kitchen and then they were shown to their small bedrooms.

Rosa and Paolo had not slept in a bed together for almost a week and they hurriedly undressed and fell into one another arms. Their passion had grown greater since that first night and their love making became so intense that it blotted out all the harrowing events of the day. They slept contentedly after, their naked bodies entwined about the other.

CHAPTER 20

The new day brought hope from an unexpected source. All three were invited to accompany Rocco on a picnic in the park where his sons and their wives and children were holding a family get-together. How good to mingle with fellow countrymen from the old country! It was a warm Indian summer day, the park was resplendent with oak and maple trees whose leaves had turned red and gold. Rosa was amazed at such beauty in the midst of the dirty city.

Introductions were made all around and Rosa, Paolo and Luigi were warmed by such congeniality. One man had brought a mandolin and another a concertina; they struck up a lively tune and soon everyone, including the children, were dancing and singing songs from home. The sons' wives had brought baskets of food and a grand feast was enjoyed.

There were roasted chickens, bowls of baked potatoes and eggplant, sliced giant tomatoes, salads mixed with fresh celery, carrots, onions, romaine, and tiny tomatoes and olives, loaves of bread baked early that morning. Dessert was watermelon, sliced into huge chunks, grapes, peaches, and plums. For the children bottles of cold apple cider were doled out in mugs, and for the men and women, wine from the cask of one of the elderly grandparents.

Rosa's eyes filled with tears as she watched the children, eating to their heart's content, laughing and singing with the adults. Her heart ached for her little brothers and sisters, their lives were so sad compared to those of Rocco's family.

Rocco explained what had transpired the day before and it was then his son, Sylvester, spoke to Paolo about the possibility of a job. "They are hiring down at the blast furnaces in the new mill, they need strong men to shovel coal all day, you look like you could handle it, Paolo," remarked Sylvester noting the huge biceps and barrel chest.

Rosa and Paolo were very excited and went to tell Luigi who had become involved in an interesting game of *bocci* with some of the older men.

The day had reaped a harvest of good fortune and that night Rosa knelt beside the bed in thanksgiving and she also prayed for the life growing in her womb.

The following day Paolo met Sylvester and they walked the two miles to the new blast furnaces. The foreman took one look at Paolo and hired him with no questions asked. In the days that followed, Paolo performed the work of three men, so eager was he to please his new employer. Each night he walked home exhausted covered with coal dust. Rosa always had water heated to bathe him, which she did in such a loving manner that Paolo would kiss her each time she bent over him. At the week's end he proudly dropped four dollars in her lap as she sat sewing the baby's layette.

"Oh, Paolo, we are going to be rich!" she said gaily.

Paolo swooped her up in his arms chanting, "*Cara mia, ti amo* (my darling, I love you)."

Sylvester wondered if they carried a sizable amount of money. They looked very poor, but appearances can sometimes be misleading, he mused. He was going to make it his business to find out.

Things had not been going well with Luigi in all this time, however. He had never been idle all his life and time fell heavily for him. The old men he had met at the picnic good naturedly encouraged him to play *bocci* with them. This was a lawn game and Luigi walked every day to the park enjoying being out of doors. He drank wine with them and soon they were boasting of his skill and how he had become so proficient at the game so quickly. One

day, Pietro Valenti, brother of Rocco, said half-jokingly,
"Hey, Luigi, once in a while we bet 20 cents on the game.
With your skill you could make some money."

Bolstered by such flattery, Luigi played, winning every game.
His pouch became heavier and each night, in the seclusion of his
room, he counted out twenty dollars he had won. He bought
cigars for his new friends, they patted him on the back and raved
over his winnings.

One day he began to lose, and questioning his losses, blamed
it on some bad food he had had the previous night, giving him
a stomach ache. He doggedly played, losing game after game.
Pietro kept urging him on saying it was just a bad streak and he
would start winning again. Soon he was betting double the stakes,
his hand trembling as he rolled the round black ball over the
lawn. His losing streak never left him and one night he realized all
his money was gone.

All his life's savings! How could he have been so foolish? How
could he tell Rosa and Paolo? Rocco had coached his brother
well. They would split the winnings between them and if the old
man had more money hidden away, he would soon lose that, too.
When Rocco realized Luigi had no more money to bet, he turned
his attention to Paolo. This would take more careful planning he
knew, for he had to deal with Rosa also.

Luigi became more despondent, staying in his room all day,
coming out only for his meals until Rosa mentioned it to Paolo
who was at the mill all day and never knew about Luigi's strange
behavior. Paolo felt it was only homesickness and it would pass
when Luigi realized Paolo was working hard every day to make a
living for them and circumstances would improve for the three of
them.

But Luigi lay upon his bed thinking of how he had labored
on his master's farm for sixty years to save forty-nine dollars and
twelve cents. This had been the culmination of his life's work, the
money he carried from Italy in his hidden pouch. Despair over-

took him; life had lost all meaning.

As he longed for the warmth of Italy, he forgot the back-breaking toil he had endured on the farm. He only knew he did not belong in this strange new world. Now he realized Paolo had begun a life of his own, with Rosa as his partner. Luigi felt like an outsider and many nights he dreamed of his wife, Anna, and his three little boys. Their faces had become dim with the passing of time. He never felt so alone.

CHAPTER 21

At the end of the month, Paolo received a grand total of sixteen dollars. He and Rosa were ecstatic! "With the two hundred dollars left from Juliana, we can now look for our own apartment, Rosa," Paolo announced.

"I can hardly believe our good fortune," Rosa answered. Then she added, "I'm worried about Luigi, he seems so strange."

"Yes, I have noticed," Paolo answered. "I think he misses Italy more then we thought."

Each Sunday after Mass, the three of them walked about the city looking for a house they could rent. Paolo was certain this would brighten Luigi who lagged behind with his head down. "See, Luigi, we will find a home of our own. You can maybe plant some vegetables for part of our meals," Paolo remarked hoping it would brighten the old man's spirit.

Luigi gave Paolo a small smile,"Yes, I would love to do some planting."

Sylvester Valenti met Paolo one day and, putting his arm over Paolo's shoulder, said, "Well, today is payday, Paolo."

"I was paid Saturday, Sylvester. This is Monday, I don't get paid again until next Saturday," Paolo said laughing.

"No, no, today is payday. You owe me twenty-four dollars," Sylvester replied, puffing on his cigar.

"Twenty-four dollars! For what?" Paolo asked in amazement.

"Six dollars a week, four weeks, twenty-four dollars," Sylvester said counting on his fingers.

"I don't understand, why do I owe you twenty-four dollars?" Paolo was confused.

"For getting you a job, *stupido*. It's twenty-four dollars a month."

"No, I will not pay," Paolo insisted.

"You'll pay, or the amount will double if you don't," the man sneered and angrily walked off.

Paolo never mentioned to Rosa what had happened or his conversation with Sylvester. His work went on uninterrupted, but as winter approached and the days grew shorter, he became apprehensive remembering Sylvester's threat. Unconsciously, he began to look over his shoulder as he walked home from work.

Two months after his encounter with Sylvester, he was met one night by three men, all carrying big sticks. "Where is the seventy-two dollars?" one snarled. "Pay up if you know what's good for you."

Paolo knew he could never be any match for three men bigger than he. When he insisted he did not have the money, they beat him badly. He lay bleeding on the ground for hours then finally staggered to the front porch where a worried Rosa stood waiting for him.

Screaming in Italian, "*DIO, DIO!* What have they done to my Paolo!" Rosa helped him to their room and onto the bed. Running for water, she bathed his bloody face and back. He told her of the threats.

"We will leave this place, Rosa," Paolo groaned through bloodied lips.

"Oh, Paolo, my Paolo!" Rosa cried. "Why have they done this terrible thing to you!"

Paolo was unable to return to the mill and stayed in their bedroom while Rosa administered to his wounds. His arm had been broken and she set it in the only fashion she knew. She told Felicia that Paolo had sprained his back and had to remain in bed.

When Paolo was able to walk, he sent for Luigi and told him they were all going to Mass together on Sunday. So deep was the old man's despair he hardly noticed Paolo's condition. Telling Rosa to gather up her coat and shawl (with the crucifix wrapped in it), they set off for church, supposedly. Every fiber of his being ached and he walked painfully. Rosa's heart cried out for the battered man she adored.

They made their way to the train station, and so as not to arouse suspicion, they left behind their few possessions. Rosa refused to leave the layette she had lovingly made and stuffed it under her dress. She had become large with child and the extra clothing would not be noticed. They bought tickets to Youngstown, a city sixty miles to the south. Their only thought was to leave this terrible place.

They arrived in Youngstown on Thanksgiving Day, a holiday unknown to them. All the stores and businesses were closed and they spent the day and night in the warm train depot, not knowing where to go. Paolo had instinctively packed bread, apples, and grapes in a compact bundle which he carried under his coat and tied to his shirt. This, carefully doled out, sustained them while using the train station as a refuge from the weather.

"Paolo, how did you know we would need the food you brought?" Rosa asked.

"Just practice, Rosa. As a boy without a home, I naturally thought things out," Paolo answered, kissing Rosa on the cheek.

Finally towards nightfall, they found a small house with a "For Rent" sign. Knocking on the door, Rosa explained to the man who answered that they wished to rent a room.

Bidding them to enter, the man introduced himself as Dr. William Raney. He peered into Paolo's still swollen face and at his bandaged arm, then looked at Rosa whom he noticed was pregnant, and said in a kindly voice, "Looks to me you folks need more than room. Here, I am a doctor, let me look at that arm, young man."

Suspicious of any kindness, Rosa replied, "It's nothing, he will be all right."

"I won't charge you anything, Missus. I think he needs some medical attention." And with that, he sat Paolo down in the nearest chair and removed the bandage.

"Needs resetting. What's your name, big fellow?" he addressed Paolo, who only looked at him in a puzzled way. Dr. Raney observed the shabby clothes of the three and took special note of the quiet and bewildered old man standing nearby, twisting a tattered scarf. After he set Paolo's arm properly, he warned him to keep his arm in a sling until it had completely healed.

Dr. Raney had been a widower for the past two years and as time went on he dreaded coming home to a dark and empty house. He decided to rent out a room, perhaps to a needy medical student. He had dealt with all kinds of people throughout his lifetime and was a keen judge of people.

He felt certain these strangers who had come to his door were good, honest folk. He felt compassion for their plight, especially for the young wife who courageously presented a happy façade in spite of her condition. Paolo assumed a brave demeanor for the sake of his wife. Luigi, who obeyed Rosa's quiet commands, seemed like a lost child.

In the days that followed, Paolo's arm began to mend and he exercised it according to the doctor's instructions until it was almost well. Rosa, in the meantime, had meekly inquired if she could cook for Dr. Raney and themselves.

"Say, I would love a woman's hand in the kitchen again. I sure am tired of my own cooking," Dr. Raney replied with enthusiasm.

Rosa cooked for the four of them and baked bread in the wood-stove's cavernous black oven. She was delighted with the tiny kitchen, and when the good doctor returned from his rounds at the hospital, he was greeted by delicious smells at the front door; he considered himself fortunate to have the young people with him.

In the evenings, Rosa tutored Paolo and gave him reading lessons from the McGuffey Reader that Dr. Raney had given her. Paolo was an apt pupil and his eagerness touched Rosa's heart.

The three of them had only one change of clothing, having left behind all they possessed. Rosa washed their clothes at night, draping them over chairs near the stove to dry. She mended and patched, trying to hold each garment intact. She found her way to a nearby butcher shop where she begged soup bones, beef heart, and kidneys, which were always discarded by butchers; these were not considered suitable human fare.

From these scraps Rosa prepared nourishing soups and stews. With Dr. Raney's permission, Paolo built a small chicken coop in the extreme back of the property. They started out with four chickens and a rooster, and soon had a supply of fresh eggs to cook for their breakfast. She and Paolo planned to plant a vegetable and herb garden that spring.

One day while cleaning the small attic, Rosa found clothing packed away very carefully in a large box. Curious, she asked, "Dr Raney, whose clothes are these?"

Dr. Raney replied, "Why, Rosa I had completely forgotten those. They belonged to Grace's father, she never wanted to give them away. Do you think you could use them?"

"I am sure we can make some over to fit Paolo and Luigi," she replied with a big smile.

Winter snows fell now, and Rosa trapped inside, kept herself busy constructing shirts for the men folk. She had never seen such heavy snow before and was grateful for the warmth of the cheerful house.

Their money was dwindling and Paolo knew he must find work. "Do you think the mills are hiring?" Paolo asked Dr. Raney one evening.

"Yes, Paolo, I believe they are. Why don't you go down tomorrow. It'll be cold, you'll need a coat." He got up from his chair and walked across the room. "I think I have a coat a patient left years ago. Big fellow like you." He brought a heavy black coat out of the armoire. "Try it on, you're welcome to it."

"Oh, Paolo, *come sei bello* (how beautiful you are)!" Paolo never looked so handsome and Rosa's eyes filled with tears. Here stood her handsome love, adorned like a merchant from Italy; her heart filled with pride.

Paolo set out for the Brier Hill Mills not far from where they lived. "This time, I do it on my own," he said to himself. I will never be obligated to anyone again. Rosa had written the word Manager in large letters on a piece of butcher paper for him to carry in his shirt pocket so he would know where to apply for a job. She had coached him to respond in English, that he had shoveled coal in the mill in Cleveland.

He had not reckoned on the cruel taunts that followed him when he arrived at the mill. He could only understand a portion of what was being hollered by a group of jeering men.

"Damn foreigners, coming to take our jobs away!"

"Hey, you big Wop, go back to the old country!"

Someone threw a piece of coal, which hit him in the back of the head. Turning angrily, he picked up the coal and threw it in the direction from which it had come. Just then a burly black man shouted, "You men! Leave him alone!" The men fell back, Roscoe Barnes was someone they feared.

Roscoe looked Paolo over from head to foot. "Looking for a job, big guy? Come with me and I'll take you to the Man." Sensing he could trust this black man, he followed him to a door marked Manager. Paolo smiled, "I never forget you," he thanked him in broken English. He was hired the following week, shoveling coal for the blast furnaces.

The Civil War had caused immense growth in the iron industry during the postwar years. Two hundred thousand tons of ore came down from the lakes in 1865; ten years later the annual cargoes exceeded half a million.

Rosa and Paolo listened attentively when Dr. Raney told them how coal had become Youngstown's greatest asset. "David Tod was the governor of Ohio in 1862. He grew up on a Brier Hill farm overlooking Youngstown, not far from my home here. The land was mostly sheep pasture, but it also contained rich coal banks, easily worked, along the Mahoning River. That coal was the best in the valley, excellent for blast furnaces. Steamboat captains who worked the river were persuaded to use coal in their boiler rooms and within ten years, coal took the place of wood for steamboat fuel."

"When did they begin making iron from coal?" Rosa asked.

"After the Civil War, Governor Tod turned to iron-making. Youngstown grew into the biggest of the mill towns: charcoal ovens, mill sheds, skip hoists, and big furnace stacks topped by smoking chimneys strung for thirty miles along the Mahoning River."

From their bedroom window Rosa could watch the blast furnaces gush white hot iron and the Bessemer converters flare in the murky sky. "Can you tell us what the converters do?" asked Paolo.

Dr. Raney was pleased Paolo and Rosa were so interested in his story. "Well, Paolo, Sir Henry Bessemer, an inventor and engineer, invented the process in 1856. I don't know if you can understand, it's a process of producing steel in which impurities are removed by forcing a blast of air through molten iron." The three laughed when Rosa and Paolo shook their heads, it was far above their minds to comprehend.

It was the Christmas season and Rosa baked Italian egg bread filled with golden raisins. The customs of gift giving and a Christmas tree were unknown in Italy. Rosa and Paolo were dumbfounded when Dr. Raney dragged home a huge fir tree, propped it up in the main room and then proceeded to decorate it with fine old ornaments stored in a huge box.

"The Missus loved Christmas," he remembered. "And she loved to decorate the tree." Excitedly, Dr. Raney said, "You two, go sit in the kitchen and I'll call you when I'm done."

Rosa and Paolo gasped in delight over the finished splendor. Tiny harps and angels hung by gossamer threads on each branch, with a shining silver cord entwined over all. Miniature candles were set at the ends of the branches; the doctor lit the candles and their glow danced off each ornament. They had never seen anything so breathtaking and they sat on the floor like children, holding hands and exclaiming over the beauty of it all. They sat there until Dr. Raney blew out the candles, and calling Merry Christmas to them, went off to bed.

The year did not end well for Luigi who grew stranger and quieter every day. Except for his meals, he never came out of his room. Dr. Raney suspected the old man was afflicted with some sort of dementia, not in any way harmful, he hoped. As anyone could see, however, Luigi was no longer in touch with the real world.

New Year's Day they found him wrapped in his blanket outside the kitchen door. He had gone to the privy in the backyard, ignoring the chamber pot under his bed, and became confused. He had fallen asleep in the snow where he froze to death. His pride had not allowed him to admit his gullibility to Paolo, or to reveal the mistake he had made that cost him his life savings. Luigi had never recovered from his shame and his secret went to the grave with him.

Paolo mourned his old friend and sorrowfully cried to Rosa that he had never bought Luigi the home he had promised. The old man had been like a father to him.

Dominic Cucco came into their world January 15, 1872. He was a healthy boy with dark hair and Paolo's blue eyes. Dr. Raney delivered the baby and gave out cigars to all his doctor friends, he was so proud. Rosa and Paolo had become like his own children, the children he and his wife never had. Rosa was a loving and devoted mother and her milk was rich and plentiful. Paolo had bought her a rocking chair and he loved to watch her nurse their hungry boy. When the baby was satisfied, he listened to Rosa sing a lullaby to him, the old familiar tune his mother had sung to him, *dormi, dormi, bambino.*

They remained with Dr. Raney. Their presence had enriched his world, he told everyone. Rosa was in the family way again, and both men watched over her anxiously this time. Things did not go well. She suffered severe morning sickness and Dr Raney became worried when all his efforts failed to provide her any relief. He was not surprised when Rosa miscarried at four months. Rosa was devastated and she cried so that Paolo wondered how he could ease her sorrow.

On his way home from the mill one day, he stopped at a small farm and purchased some rose bushes. Perhaps their bloom would bring a smile to Rosa's face as they had at Castello del Sole.

CHAPTER 22

Dominic was now walking and loved being with his Papa. As Paolo dug holes in the backyard for the roses, Dominic got a little stick and stood digging beside his father. Looking out the kitchen window Rosa spied the two of them and her heart was so full of love, she ran out of the house and threw her arms around Paolo. She vowed to put the unhappy few months behind her and she rejoiced in her blessings.

When Dominic was three years old, Rosa gave birth to Lucia, a tiny image of herself. Paolo was so enraptured with his little daughter, that he held her every spare moment. She was his *carissima mia* and he whispered it over and over in her tiny ear. Dominic watched over his baby sister devotedly. When she began to talk at an early age, she had difficulty pronouncing his name and it always came out "Nick." Her favorite toy was a cloth doll Rosa had fashioned from scraps left over from Dominic's shirts and pants.

"Why do you call me *carissima mia*, Papa?"she would ask.

"Because you are my sweetheart," he would answer. It became a little joke between them.

The doctor's house seemed to grow smaller and smaller with the arrival of each new child and Paolo asked Dr. Raney if he could build an addition onto the rear of the house. Dr. Raney was delighted. Every evening after work, Paolo sawed boards and pounded nails until, just in time, the room was completed and Antonio was born, named after Rosa's father,

Dominic was ready to enter first grade at public school and Rosa proudly registered him, explaining to the teacher that she and Dominic read from the McGuffey Reader every day. Lucia begged to "go schoo" with Dominic, and Rosa had a difficult time keeping her from following her brother into class every day. Until he felt secure in his new environment, Dominic and his Mama walked the two blocks to school, Lucia and Antonio in tow. His teacher, Miss Sutton, was quite surprised, not only with Rosa's fluent English, which by this time had only a slight accent, but also with the determination she expressed regarding her son's education.

Dominic was the brightest of all her pupils and had shown such aptitude in all his subjects that it was not long before he was reading at the third grade level. A Christmas play was on the program for the holiday season and Dominic was chosen to act the part of St. Joseph. Every evening after dinner Dominic and Rosa acted out the play, to the amusement of Paolo; Lucia clapped her little hands every time Dominic recited his lines.

Christmas that year was the happiest for the Cucco family. Paolo had become Assistant Manager, under Roscoe Barnes who recommended Paolo for the position. Never had Roscoe encountered a more willing worker, the men who had taunted Paolo learned to respect him. When a man became ill or was unable to work, Paolo visited the family with baskets of food. Rosa also helped, as she remembered how desperate her young brothers and sisters were many years ago. A loaf of bread and cookies were also in the delivered basket. Rosa gave thanks for all her blessings. She regularly attended Mass at St. Joseph's, a church founded by the Italian immigrants

She volunteered what little time she had to help the good women of the Altar Society, who held monthly fund-raising dinners for the church. She made lifelong friends with many of these devoted hard-working women, especially Georgina Massini, who would become *comare* to the Cucco children.

It was during the following year an epidemic spawned a growing menace called influenza. Frightened parents kept their children home from school. Dominic begged to be allowed to go, and despite misgivings, Rosa consented. The dreaded disease spread, however, and panic gripped the hearts of the people. Dr. Raney treated patients twenty hours of the day, falling asleep at the dinner table.

"You must keep Dominic home Rosa," Dr. Raney warned. "I am asking the superintendent to close all schools." His warning came too late. Dominic awoke the following day with a raging fever. Soon Lucia and Antonio were sick, Rosa was frantic and hardly slept, ministering to her children night and day, until Paolo found her one evening on the floor exhausted and carried her to bed. He took up the vigil, allowing Rosa a few hours rest, and when she awakened, the two knelt beside their children's beds, applying wet cloths to their fevered brows. Her tears fell un-checked as she bathed each child with cool water.

All their efforts were to no avail. Antonio breathed his last in the early dawn the following day. Lucia raised a tiny hand to Paolo's face, then closed her eyes forever. Paolo's grief was heart-rending, his huge body racked by sobs. He and Rosa clung together as the two tiny caskets sat side by side in the main room. Mourning friends tried to console the grief-stricken parents. Roscoe Barnes and his wife were there, even though, they too, had lost a child the week before. The sound of weeping filled the room.

Dominic survived, but the terrible fever had wrought hav-oc with his brain. Gone was his reading and learning ability; he remained at home with Rosa as his teacher. Each day she worked patiently with her young son, who had become listless and disin-terested.

Her heart was heavy with the loss of Lucia and Antonio. The challenge of restoring Dominic's mind seemed impossible and she almost gave up hope. Each day the chore became more difficult. She knew Dominic missed his brother and sister, and one day she found him with Lucia's favorite doll, hugging it to him, crying *carissima mia* over and over.

Rosa and Paolo sought the advice of Father Andrew, the parish priest. "Perhaps a change of scenery would do him a world of good," he advised.

Rosa's friend, Georgina, offered to take the boy to summer camp. The young lad half-heartedly packed a small satchel and set off on the train with his godmother.

Geneva-on-the-Lake was a lovely spot on the south side of Lake Erie. Young boys gathered here during the summer to swim and hike. Supervised boating, nature walks and outdoor activities kept the boys busy. After the first few days, Dominic lost his shyness and began to join in the fun. When he came home, he was once again smiling and playing with his neighborhood friends. He returned to school, but work was laborious and his best efforts achieved only an average grade. Rosa continued to work with him every night urging him to do his best.

CHAPTER 23

*D*uring the next five years, Roscoe helped Paolo and Rosa enlarge the nursery, as the family was growing again. In the Fall of the year 1883, Maria was born, twins Giorgio and Guisepppe made their debut in 1885, and little Vincenzo surprised the family two years later, December 1887.

Paolo and Rosa's family had become as Dr. Raney's own. They called him "Papa Will" and their love meant more to him than anything. As the years wore on, his heart gave a twinge now and then. He found himself growing tired and missing his departed Grace. Evenings, he would fall asleep with her photo in his hand.

Grace had been a patient and devoted wife, sacrificing small pleasures to help him complete medical school. Dr. Raney drew up a will, leaving the house and a plot of land adjacent to Rosa and Paolo. His small savings was set aside as a college fund for worthy medical students. The day before his seventieth birthday, Will Raney gently went to sleep in his favorite chair, Grace's picture slipping from his hand.

The plot of land Dr. Raney bequeathed was vacant and Paolo had visions of building a large home for his family. With the help of several church members and Roscoe, the new house began to take shape.

"We are going to have indoor plumbing," Paolo announced one evening, "and we're going to pipe in gas for lighting."

"Can we have such luxuries, Paolo?" Rosa asked.

"There is no rush to build the house," Paolo replied. "We will have it right and the way we want, even if it takes a little longer to complete."

Rosa inspected the work every day. The children ran through the house shouting, "Which room is mine, Mama?"

At the front of the house, a heavy oak door opened into a long entryway, with a large parlor to the right, which could be closed off by sliding doors. Stairs on the left led up to four bedrooms, each having two dormer windows. A beveled-glass French door at the end of the entry opened into a dining room and beyond, a spacious kitchen.

There was a sewing room for Rosa off the dining room with a lovely bay window looking out into the fenced backyard. Built into the upstairs hallway were shelves and drawers for linen storage, and at the head of the stairs, a door opened into the attic. The big house included a huge cellar, along one side of which Paolo had built a dozen shelves for Rosa's jars of home canned food. On the opposite side, Paolo had built a work bench for himself.

Perhaps the grandest feature of the entire house was the brick fireplace in the dining room. This was to be the focal point of the home, where the family gathered in the evenings, where Paolo could read his evening paper and smoke his pipe while Rosa studied with the children.

Roscoe insisted on laying cement over a period of three weekends. He created four stone steps at the entrance to the house with a curving balustrade on either side. When he laid a walkway from the steps to the street, all the neighbors exclaimed over the beauty of the finished workmanship.

Moving day finally arrived and the children were so excited, carrying their own little treasures to their respective rooms. Rosa gave Maria her own room, the twins shared a room, and Dominic and Vincenzo were in another leaving Rosa and Paolo a room all their own, which was a pleasant change. A baby crib had occupied their bedroom all these years and Rosa was delighted to have space where she could place the lovely armoire Papa Will had left them.

Dominic loved having Vincenzo in his room. Since Lucia's

death he never wanted to sleep alone and kept his little brother's crib close to his own bed so he could peer over each morning and watch the baby's quiet breathing. He tended Vincenzo, who padded after him all day that summer and when Dominic was off to school, Vinnie would watch at the front window for his return.

Rosa studied American History that year in preparation for her American citizenship. She tutored Paolo and at the end of that year, they became American citizens. Their children and neighbors held a party for them and Rosa hung an American flag from the front porch declaring their pride of citizenship; it was 1890.

Rosa had written many letters to her benefactress, Contessa Juliana de Salvatore, each one returned with 'address unknown' stamped across the envelope. This deeply grieved Rosa and she could not understand why the letters had not been forwarded. She hoped Juliana was well and wondered whether Damien was still living with her. She and Paolo often asked themselves these questions, for it was because of her they came to America and their lives so changed dramatically over the years.

Many nights as she and Paolo lay in bed they gave thanks to Juliana, always with the same words, "Can you believe all that has happened to us in the past years, Paolo?"

"I know what you are saying, Rosa," he would reply. "Who would have thought we would be citizens of such a great country. Each morning when I awaken and see you lying beside me, I think back on those hard times in Italy and the thought of no future."

Rosa now began to invite friends over once a month for dinner and a game of cards. Their favorite game was called "Michigan." Played with two decks of cards, any number of people could play. The older children loved to be included and squealed with delight when one of them would win. Roscoe and his wife, Amelia, and their four children were often their guests.

Rosa did not believe in gambling and forbade any show of money. When Michigan was played at the home of Georgina and her husband, Ugo, they always had a huge jar filled with pennies that they sold to the players. "It makes the game more fun, Rosa," Georgina insisted.

"I don't want the children to learn any bad habits," Rosa defended.

"Oh, heck, Rosa, what's a few pennies going to hurt," Ugo answered.

But when the pennies appeared, Rosa insisted the children play "Go Fish" in the kitchen.

The men teased Paolo, saying Rosa was the boss in his home, Paolo good-naturedly answered, "Rosa is a good mother, I respect her wishes." His remarks were always followed by a smile and a wink. The men soon learned that Paolo never took any of their teasing seriously, and the women admired him for the love he showed Rosa.

Occasionally the men gathered for a game of poker all by themselves. Paolo never went over the limit of five dollars. When that amount was gone, he excused himself from the table. He and Rosa had worked too hard for their small savings and he was not about to squander it in a game of cards.

On those nights when the men gathered for poker, George and Joseph (the twins had adopted the American version of their names) were interested spectators. They watched the game quietly, never saying a word. In their own room, they re-enacted the poker game. They memorized cards, always testing one another. They taught themselves the fine art of keeping their faces absolutely blank, as do all good poker players. This was their secret.

CHAPTER 24

The years went by swiftly. Maria turned fourteen and entered Rayen High School on the north side of Youngstown. Colonel William Rayen, a judge and former military officer who fought in the War of 1812, provided a legacy to create the school, which he insisted would blend the cultures of the wealthy, the middle class and the poor. Maria fell into the middle class category and was a little ashamed of her Italian background. However, she was fiercely proud of her parents, her tall, handsome father and her petite dark-eyed mother. But she longed to be a part of the young American class and because of this she hated her foreign sounding name of Cucco.

"What does Cucco mean, Papa?" she inquired one night.

"It means Cook," Paolo answered.

"Why can't we use that name, Papa? It sounds American," she insisted.

"Don't you be ashamed of your Italian heritage!"Rosa snapped, annoyed.

"But, Mama, you're American now and you should have an American name."

Paolo finally consented and Maria was overjoyed when she could sign her name, Marie Anne Cook.

Massillon, Ohio was the birthplace of women's rights in Ohio and Oberlin College was the first coeducational college in America. Rosa dreamed of Marie attending Oberlin and encouraged her constantly as her daughter had a quick and inquiring mind. Rosa subscribed to the journal, *Woodhull and Claflin's Weekly*, which advocated equal rights for women.

Marie had inherited her mother's love of books and was intent on getting a good education. Her schedule for the junior year was ambitious, to say the least, and included Latin, English literature, biology and algebra. As usual, the first day of the new semester was hectic. Her best friend, Susan Fields, had the same classes, and as they went from class to class, they compared notes, on teachers, subjects and boys.

They entered their algebra class and, seating themselves in the back of the room, proceeded to take inventory of their class-mates. Suddenly, the door opened and a tall, good looking young man entered, walked to the blackboard and wrote his name, Mr. Palumbo. Then taking a pointer and placing it under his name, turned and addressed the class.

"I am Mr. Palumbo and the game plan for this year is to learn algebra."

"Sounds like he's going to teach us football," snickered one of the boys in a low voice.

"Football?" Marie whispered.

"Sure, he's the new assistant football coach."

As the algebra books were passed out, Susan gushed, "Isn't he handsome!"

Marie was so taken with the new teacher she could not con-centrate on the example Mr. Palumbo had written on the board. She fumbled with her papers and dropped her books, which creat-ed such a disturbance that her new teacher frowned at her.

"How could I be so clumsy!" she exploded to Susan after class.

"Well, you got him to notice you." Susan smirked.

"Sure, he probably thinks I'm the class idiot," Marie pouted.

The next few weeks were difficult for Marie. For the first time in her school years, she could not comprehend this new subject. Algebra frustrated her. Mr. Palumbo had called on her to give an answer and she could not.

"Marie, what's wrong with you?" Susan asked after class.

"I can't understand it myself," Marie answered, biting her lip.

Marie went about the house the next few days so downcast that her brother George asked her teasingly, tossing a football in the air, "Hey, Sis, lost your last friend?"

"Oh, leave me alone!" she retorted.

"Just trying to be friendly. Say, would you like to come to football practice Saturday and watch your brothers' team? Your new algebra teacher will be there."

"Damien?" Marie asked, amazed.

"Yeah, he's our coach, you know."

"Oh, George, you're the best brother ever! Of course I'll come to your practice," and she threw her arms about her surprised brother.

Marie could hardly wait for Saturday and spent hours trying to decide what to wear. She discarded sweaters and coats, blouses and skirts, fussed with her hair, and finally picked out a navy skirt with tiny buttons down the front, topped by a plain white silk blouse. Over this she wore a long knit sweater jacket of navy with flecks of red barely visible in the yarn. She tied her long, wavy black hair in a red bow at the back and pinched her cheeks until they were a healthy pink.

When she appeared, George and Joseph let out long whistles, surprised at their sister's good looks. The three set off for the practice fields. The day was sunny with a bit of a cold wind blowing. Marie pretended to be very interested in the game, all he while looking for Damien Palumbo. When she saw him, she stood up and waved to her brothers, hoping the handsome coach would see her. He never even noticed. The sun went behind a cloud and she began to feel uncomfortable with the cold air blowing her hair about. Not wanting to leave, but becoming more chilled by the minute, she called to George who came running over.

"I'm going home, I'm freezing," Marie wailed.

"Gosh, Sis, I guess it is cold sitting out here. I'll see you later," he said apologetically.

Marie walked home as fast as she could, angry and disappointed. That night she developed a sore throat and Rosa heated camphorated oil to rub on Marie's neck and made hot chamomile tea. Worry lines creased Rosa's forehead and she and Paolo fussed over her all night.

"Gee, Mama, she only has a little sore throat," Giorgio said disgustedly.

"You should never have asked her to sit out in that cold air," Rosa snapped.

The memory of losing Lucia and Antonio to influenza tortured Rosa and she would not leave Marie all night, sitting by her bed until dawn. By morning Marie had no temperature, just a slight tickle in her throat, but Rosa would not let her get out of bed. Paolo gave orders she was to remain in bed until Rosa gave her permission to get up.

"So much fuss, Mama, I'm okay now," Marie said.

"You are to stay in bed. Your father will not tolerate any disobedience," Rosa said sternly, hoping to impress Marie with an order from higher up.

Marie was absent from school for two days, still in bed and feeling miserable, piqued with her parents. She wore an old faded bathrobe and books and papers were strewn across the bed. A white cotton sock soaked in camphorated oil was pinned around her neck. She heard her brothers running up the stairs, then George and Joseph poked their heads in the door.

"Have a visitor for you, Marie."

And with that they showed her algebra teacher, Damien Palumbo, into the room. Marie wanted to crawl under the covers and disappear forever.

"Missed you at class, Marie. I've brought your assignments. Sure was nice of you to come to practice. Most girls wouldn't even bother." Damien said, smiling.

"Oh, yes, I loved it," Marie lied. "But I had to get home to write an essay for English Lit."

She pulled off the offending sock and smoothed her tousled

hair. I'll kill those brothers of mine, she vowed. How could they do this to me?

"Will you come to the game next week, Marie?" Damien asked.

She could hardly believe her ears. He was really asking her to go to the game! Her heart skipped several beats, but she answered matter-of-factly, trying not to reveal her excitement, "If I get feeling better, Mr. Palumbo."

Damien and the twins went downstairs. Rosa heard the door close with a loud bang. Certain the boys had left, Marie jumped up and down on the bed, laughing and letting out little bleeps of excitement. Rosa came running upstairs with all the commotion.

"What happened, Marie! Are you all right?" she asked anxiously.

"Oh, yes, Mama, I'm fine," Marie answered happily, "I'll stay in bed all day today as you asked and maybe tomorrow I'll come downstairs and help you bake bread." Giving her mother a hug and a kiss, she straightened up her bed, got down under the covers and began conjuring up delicious dreams about Damien.

As Rosa was leaving the room, after having seen only the back of the blond young man with the twins, she asked Marie, "Who was that young man with your brothers?"

"Oh, that's the new assistant football coach, Mama. His name is Damien Palumbo."

Rosa's head came up sharply. Damien? Could it be?

"What do you know about him, Marie?" Rosa asked, interested now.

"Nothing much. He's my algebra teacher. George says his father is an artist and they live on Fifth Avenue in one of those big houses." Marie wondered why her mother was suddenly so interested.

"I think I'll take a nap now," she said, hoping her mother would leave so she could relish the events of the past half hour.

CHAPTER 25

*R*osa remembered Juliana telling her about Elena's journal, in which she spoke of the artist, Leo Palumbo. He was the father of Damien and also the artist who painted Elena's portrait. She recalled Elena, in the throes of her delivery, whispering to Rosa, that Leo was the father of her child. She quietly vowed to speak to Paolo when he returned from the mill.

Rosa's curiosity over Damien surprised her children, she had never seemed so interested in their teachers before. Rosa mulled over in her head so many unanswered questions. If he was Elena's son, how could he have turned up in Youngstown?

She meant to find out and requested the twins invite him to dinner after the next game. Marie was puzzled at her mother's behavior, but said nothing for fear of spoiling a wonderful opportunity to be with Damien.

Saturday came and even though the day was warm, Rosa insisted Marie wear a hat and scarf. Rosa had never seen Marie so excited and promised to have a delicious dinner waiting for their return. Rayon school defeated their opponents and it was a cheerful, noisy group that tramped boisterously into the house.

"Boy! What smells so good, Mama?" asked George planting a kiss on Rosa's cheek. The minestrone had been simmering on the stove's back burner all day long. There was a loaf of homemade bread cut in thick slices, placed in the center of the table.

"Get washed up children, ordered Rosa. "George, introduce your teacher to Papa." Paolo had been standing by greatly amused by the comaraderie of the young people.

"Papa, this is Damien Palomba, the new assistant football coach," he smiled. "His strategy helped win the game."

"Well, that's quite a tribute, Damien. I am happy to make your acquaintance," said Paolo shaking hands with the young man, who blushed at George's praise.

Marie was ecstatic and the dinner was even more than she had hoped for. Her mother was a marvelous cook and Rosa had outdone herself. The twins gulped down their food despite Rosa's protests. "Leave some for someone else," she scolded.

"He who eats the fastest gets the most," they replied in unison.

Damien commented he had not had such a delicious meal since his late grandmother cooked for him.

"Thank you, Damien," replied Rosa. "And where did your grandmother live?"

"She lived in Italy, a city called Bari, in the Apulia region. That's where I'm from," answered Damien, his mouth full of cake.

"When did you come to America?" Paolo inquired, not wanting Rosa to ask all the questions.

"Oh, I left Italy in 1882 when I was twelve years old when my grandmother died. My mother died when I was born, I never knew her, but I have paintings of her my father gave me," he answered.

The questioning went no farther as the boys interrupted and began going over the game play by play. Paolo motioned to Rosa to discontinue her line of conversation and politely listened to the boys and Marie expounding the merits of the game. When Damien finally took his leave, after thanking Rosa and Paolo for a delicious meal, Marie ran upstairs to her room in a happy state of mind. Everything had gone so well

Damien had been so attentive to her on the way home and Mama had invited him back! What had come over her mother? Marie had been so proud of her parents. Papa made a handsome figure in his Sunday suit and Mama had worked all day making the meal special.

Damien had no romantic interest in Marie, she was only a child. Visiting her at her home was merely a kindness. He was a lonely man, twenty-seven years old, and he longed to be part of an Italian family again. He liked the Cook twins and the moment he stepped inside their family home, felt comfortable, as though he belonged there.

His father's home was far more grand, lavish would describe it more accurately. Damien always felt like a stranger there. When his father, Leo, had sent for him after the death of his grand-mother, Damien felt like he was meeting a reluctant relative. Leo never embraced his son, and as to Damien's arrival in America, a handshake was his only greeting.

One afternoon Rosa and her friend Georgina Massini walked into the downtown section of Youngstown. McKelvey's Department Store had just opened and they were anxious to walk through such a prestigious store. She and Georgina chatted all the while, exclaiming over the lovely merchandise. Moving on they walked down Federal Street where two new shops had also opened.

"One is an art studio," Rosa exclaimed, stopping before the front window of the studio, staring at a large painting displayed on a tall easel.

"Rosa, what's wrong? You look like you've seen a ghost," cried Georgina clutching Rosa's arm.

"It's Elena!" gasped Rosa, still staring at the painting. "Damien is Elena's son!"

Pushing a very puzzled Georgina into the store, Rosa approached the store clerk and inquired about the artist of the love-ly painting in the window.

"The artist is Leo Palumbo," answered the clerk in response to Rosa's question.

"Who was the model?" asked Rosa.

"I have a brochure here somewhere, Madam, if you will be patient, I will find it," commented the clerk.

"Why on earth, are you so interested, Rosa."

"I'll explain later, Georgina. Here comes the clerk."

The clerk produced a small brochure which Rosa read eagerly:

> The artist, Leo Palumbo, an Italian, painted the portrait titled, "Madelaine," in 1871. It is believed his wife was the model.

Thanking the clerk, Rosa pushed Georgina out the door.

"Tell me what this is all about before I explode!" admonished Georgina.

"Let's find a quiet spot and I'll tell you," answered Rosa, her face all flushed with excitement.

A small tea room type restaurant had recently opened near the town square and the two ladies entered, seated themselves, and ordered tea and biscuits, then settled in for a long conversation.

Knowing Georgina to be a prudent listener, Rosa started at the very beginning revealing her past association with Juliana, Elena and Reno. Georgina listened with amazement, never having heard the story before and when Rosa spoke of Damien living in Youngstown could only exclaim,"There's no question, Rosa. He is Elena's son."

"But why did they come to Youngstown and why is Leo pretending Elena was his wife, and what happened to Juliana?" Rosa wondered out loud.

"It's an intriguing mystery and I'm sure you are going to find out," said Georgina with finality in her voice.

CHAPTER 26

*P*aolo was now forty-seven years old and had steadily risen up the ranks at Brier Hill Mill. He had averted a strike in the mill, mostly through his efforts working with management and representing the mill workers, who had tremendous faith in him. They knew him to be a fair minded, steady man, one who never shirked any job and was always ready to work overtime or help out a friend.

He became foreman and with that position could afford to send Dominic to college if he so desired. But the young lad had his mind set on entering St. John's Seminary in preparation for the priesthood, much to Rosa's delight. Paolo had watched him struggle through the years, his quiet withdrawal after the deaths of Lucia and Antonio. Dominic would never permit anyone to call him Nick, as that was the name Lucia had given him.

Dominic's learning abilities had returned and he spent hours in his room reading. He helped Rosa about the house never permitting her to do any heavy lifting or scrubbing; he watched over Vinnie in such a fatherly way that the young boy went to him for advice or help, which slightly wounded Paolo.

Paolo's love for Rosa had never diminished over the years, if anything it had grown stronger. Rosa was a devoted wife and mother and a great sense of pride to him. He was in the prime of his life and when he looked at his family at mealtime, was proud to be the patriarch of such a loving and handsome family.

He had reached complete enrichment of his life and at Mass on Sunday bowed his head in thanksgiving. It came as a complete surprise, however, when Rosa informed him, with a sigh of happiness in her voice, that at forty-three years old, she was again with child. Rosa had always loved children and this one, she told Paolo, would crown her role as wife and mother.

Meanwhile, bolstered with a glowing reference from Father Andrew of St. Joseph's, Dominic applied for entry into St. John's Seminary. After many written examinations and several audiences with the admitting counselors, he was admitted as a seminarian in the Catholic faith. In the ensuing months, Dominic knew he had found his life's work and a peace never experienced pervaded his whole being. For the first three months he was not permitted to visit family. Vinnie sorely missed Dominic and slowly turned back to Paolo for comfort, which was accepted with gratitude and fatherly love.

During the ensuing months, Marie's fascination for Damien grew and it appeared he returned her interest, inviting her to every game after which they either returned to the Cook home for dinner or stopped at a malt shop always accompanied by her brothers, George and Joseph.

It had been a glorious Fall and as Christmas time approached Damien informed the Cook family he would be spending the holidays with friends. Marie was downcast as she had envisioned holiday parties, decorating the Christmas tree, ice-skating on the lake, all with Damien. Rosa had noticed her daughter's preoccupation with Damien and suggested to Paolo they plan a huge Christmas dinner with friends and families from the church.

The plan met with little enthusiasm from Marie, but seeing her mother's excitement she was drawn into the spirit of the coming festivities. Marie had been embarrassed when she learned of her mother's pregnancy; she never gave a thought her parents might still engage in sex, presuming all such activity ceased years ago.

Rosa had planned with Georgina to invite families who had sons Marie's age, and much conspiracy went on between the two of them until Paolo laughingly whispered in Rosa's ear one night what she had in mind. Georgina discovered there were two families in the parish with seventeen- and eighteen-year-old sons. Ugo

Massini, Georgina's husband, suggested they invite his nephew, Frank, who would be home from college during the holiday season.

Dominic was permitted by the Archdiocese to spend four days during Christmas with his family, and Vinnie decorated the bedroom he and Dominic had shared. But Dominic was quiet and withdrawn, shutting himself away from family, reading and praying all the while, barely noticing his brother's efforts. Vinnie was sorely unhappy at this turn of evens and in his disappointment, asked Marie if he could help her decorate the house. Marie was pleasantly surprised and the unusual sound of Marie and Vinnie laughing as they worked together gladdened Rosa's heart.

Party day arrived and the aroma of delicious foods and baked confections greeted the arriving guests. The Italian-American Christmas Eve dinner was called "The Feast of the Seven Fishes" and true to its name, seven types of fish were served. Smelts dipped into an egg and flour mixture were fried to a crispy brown. Dried salt cod was soaked in water for an entire day, then cut up into small pieces and boiled to make a soup mixed with potatoes, green beans, chick peas, and tomatoes. Eel, shrimp, anchovies and sardines were also served. Calamari fried to a crisp was Paolo's favorite.

The twins gulped their food down to Rosa's cries of protest, "Save some for someone else!" she scolded.

Their reply was always the same: "He who eats the fastest gets the most."

After the meal the left-over food was set out on the table and covered with a clean, white cloth and another place set. This was an old tradition carried over for generations in the chance an unfortunate should come by in need of a meal.

The boys had rolled up the carpets in the parlor, Ugo had brought his concertina and after the sumptuous banquet, everyone sang and danced. Marie had shown little interest in the two teen-age boys that had accompanied their parents, much to Rosa's dismay. Marie had just finished a lively dance with Paolo when the doorbell rang and running to the door, face flushed from the dance, opened it to find a young man with a package in one hand and his hat in the other.

"Hello, is this the Cook house? I'm Frank Massini, my Uncle Ugo invited me to your party. I'm sorry to be late, but the train was delayed."

Extending her hand in greeting, Marie drew him into the house saying, "Please come in, I'm Marie." Gone were any thoughts of Damien as she looked into dark eyes that did not disguise their admiration. Just then Paolo entered and with great cordiality invited Frank to come in and join the others.

"This is for Mrs. Cook, sir," handing the package to Paolo.

"I'm sure she will be pleased. Have you eaten yet?" asked Paolo who noted Marie seemed at a loss for words.

"No, sir, and I'm starved," answered Frank.

"Marie, fill up a plate for this young man while I introduce him around," Paolo commanded.

"Yes, Papa," answered Marie, hurrying to do her father's bidding piling a plate high. Quickly, she returned where Frank was being greeted by Georgina and Ugo.

"You've given me enough food for several days, Marie, thank you," Frank said smiling revealing a large dimple in his left cheek.

Glancing at the two of them, Rosa went back in time, remembering her first encounter with Paolo. It had been a magical, golden moment, a memory she kept tucked away in her heart untarnished by time. This is what her woman's intuition sensed when she saw what passed between Marie and Frank. Rosa felt Frank might be a man who had the ambition and perseverance to complete his studies and become a successful person. This is the man for my Marie, she had already decided, and would inform Paolo that very night.

The party was a huge success and the holiday season ended on a happy note. Frank promised to write Marie from college and she happily replied she would answer his letters. Dominic eagerly returned to the seminary and only Vincenzo was disappointed with the outcome of the holidays and the lack of attention from Dominic. He asked the twins if he could practice football with them. They were more than enthused and the team welcomed the newcomer who in time had the makings of a good athlete.

Rosa had not been able to learn anything more from Damien and not wanting to appear overly inquisitive, ceased her questioning of the boy. But somehow she would uncover the secret if only for her own satisfaction.

May 25, 1898, Rosa gave birth for the last time, naming her new daughter, Philomena, in memory of Paolo's little sister who had died in the earthquake. This was a quiet child who was content to play in her crib for hours, never making a disturbance, a tiny smile lighting her sweet face when a member of the family approached her. Paolo could not resist this gentle child, it was almost as though Lucia had come back to him. When she learned to walk, she waddled after Paolo when he was home from work and loved to climb up on his lap while he read the evening paper.

Part Three:
A NEW CENTURY

CHAPTER 27

The year 1900 seemed bright with promise. Dominic found happiness in the seminary, the twins had gone into the oil business, working for the Marathon Oil Company in Findlay. Vinnie had won a football scholarship to Notre Dame where he was studying to become an architect.

Marie graduated from high school, took a business course, and was now employed in the office of Republic Steel. Marie and Frank announced their engagement that summer, with plans to marry after Frank graduated college, much to the family approval.

Rosa learned that Damien was in Cleveland, the mystery not yet solved but one she vowed to unravel one day. With only one small child at home, Rosa now had time to study; she planted a small seed in her mind that one day she would get a high school diploma and enter college. It was a dream she had never shared with anyone.

When they moved into the bigger house, Rosa and Paolo rented out the smaller house left to them by Dr. Raney. After Marie and Frank's engagement, with Marie's wedding date drawing near, Rosa suggested the couple consider renting the smaller house. The rent was eight dollars a month, a price Rosa felt Frank could afford.

Marie had mixed emotions about such a move. On the one hand it would be comforting to be near her parents, yet on the other hand she did not want any family interference. She was not as concerned with her father, it was her mother she was worried about. Rosa had always treated Marie like a child and in spite of the girl's protest that she be allowed to make her own decisions, somehow it seemed Rosa always got the upper hand.

Poor Rosa! Her whole life had been in the service of others, she knew no other way. Her love for Paolo and her children encompassed her whole being. She doted on Philomena who remained unspoiled in spite of her mother's constant attention. Her energy seemed limitless and her days were filled with dusting and cleaning, washing and ironing. She was a marvelous cook paying extreme attention to the health of her family. Her nights were special, she read constantly, devouring books loaned from the new library four blocks from her home. She was active in the church diligently baking cakes and breads for dinners and bake sales.

Frank Massini had graduated from college and planned on becoming a certified public accountant, a career that needed two more years of schooling. He calculated he could work days for his Uncle Ugo, who had gone into business and had invested in a hot air furnace fueled by coal, and go to night school so that he and Marie could get married. Marie was delighted and in spite of Rosa's protests, began making preparations for a simple wedding.

"Don't get involved, Rosa," admonished Paolo.

"But Paolo, I only want a beautiful wedding for Marie," answered Rosa.

"Do you remember our wedding?" Paolo said quietly.

"Yes, Paolo, I will never forget it." Rosa said with a sigh and a hint of tears in her eyes.

"It was what you wanted, simple as it was," reminded Paolo. "Marie should be allowed her own way."

"You are right, my love. I needed to be reminded," said Rosa reaching up to kiss him.

Marie had her way, she was married at St. Joseph's Church and was a radiant bride. Father Andrew celebrated a Nuptial Mass with Dominic as co-celebrant. Her friend, Susan Fields, was her maid of honor. Jimmie Massini, Frank's cousin, was best man. Paolo proudly gave her away, making a handsome picture; Philomena was a delightful flower girl, daintily sprinkling rose petals down the aisle.

A huge family reception, with all the Cook and Massini families present, was held at the Cook home and lasted until the wee hours of the morning. Marie and Frank had quietly slipped away early to the little house next door.

"Do you think your mother might walk in on us, sweetheart?" teased Frank.

"She won't be able to, Papa changed the locks," giggled Marie.

Frank threw back his head and let out a huge roar. Then reaching for Marie, pulled her down on the bed.

"You'd better get out of that damn dress soon or I will tear it off."

"No, you won't! I'm saving it for our daughter some day," pouted Marie. "You just sit there and watch me undress."

Frank sat on the bed and impatiently watched his bride undress, folding each garment neatly over a chair. When the precious gown and ruffled slip came off, Frank could endure it no longer and threw Marie down on the bed.

"You little vixen, teasing me that way," he murmured passionately, his face buried in her hair.

Marie began to giggle and hiccup. "See what you did, getting me all excited," she gasped between hiccups.

"Are you excited, Marie?" he was tender now, and slowly removed all of her clothes until she lay naked before him.

"Tell me you love me, say it please darling," she whispered still hiccuping.

"I love you, my black-haired vixen, I love you," and as he kissed her hard her hiccups stopped.

They made love all night and slept until almost noon. The house was quiet and no one disturbed them from next door. Papa probably gave orders, laughed Marie, and then felt guilty for when they went into the kitchen found enough food for a week left by Rosa. They never left the house for three days, this was the honeymoon they wanted, just being together.

CHAPTER 28

*A*way from Dominic's sobering shadow, Vincenzo blossomed and cut a dashing figure off-campus. His tall good looks and flashing smile broke many a young girl's heart. Hoping to make some extra money during summer break, he went to work for Frank's Uncle Ugo at the Holland Furnace Company.

He and Frank made a two-man team and when Vinnie discovered how easily he could sell furnace cleaning orders, he dashed about, jumping over fences eager to canvas every home on the street. Frank good-naturedly walked alongside his ambitious brother-in-law and was soon learning to sell furnaces.

Ugo Massini urged the two young men to stay on with him guaranteeing them a good livelihood in the furnace business. But Vincenzo declined, eager to get his degree and make good his scholarship, with the promise he would return the following summer. Frank stayed on, realizing he could fare greatly in this exciting enterprise. Marie was in complete agreement with her husband as their finances had never looked better.

Christmas was a noisy holiday with the Cook family invited to share Christmas Eve dinner with the Massini's who numbered ten children, eleven grandchildren and scores of aunts and uncles. The Massini home was by far the largest on the street consisting of two main parlors, a dining room of tremendous size, a kitchen and magnificent sun porch. The upstairs boasted seven bedrooms all of which were constantly full.

Rosa and Paolo left after dinner as Philomena wanted to go home fearing Santa Claus would miss their house if she was not there. After dinner, Marie and Frank made the announcement they were to be parents next summer, much to the joy of both families.

"Our first grandchild, my love," said Rosa emotionally as they walked through the snow towards home.

Carrying Philomena in his arms he answered, "Yes, little one, and I hope Marie is as wonderful a mother as you have been."

Squeezing his arm tighter, they walked slowly on, snow-flakes drifting softly down creating a picture more lovely than any painting. They entered the house, fragrant with the smell of pine emanating from the decorated Christmas tree. Paolo carried Philomena upstairs letting her know they were home and that Santa would soon come. Rosa undressed a very sleepy little girl, pulled the covers over her, then stooping, kissed the soft cheek.

Returning downstairs where Paolo was waiting, Rosa turned down the gas lights and they sat side by side, the moon casting a soft glow over the Christmas tree with its gleaming ornaments and shining strands of imitation pearls strung by Rosa with the help of Marie.

"Have you been happy Paolo?" asked Rosa as she leaned against his arm.

"Luigi told me my dream was an omen of good things to come, and he was right. As a boy in Italy, I never thought my life could be so happy," he answered emotionally, cupping her face in his hand and kissing her softly on the lips.

Marie had a difficult pregnancy and in her discomfort was impatient with Frank who had been staying out late at night, working as his excuse. It was true he was bringing home more money than Marie had ever seen before, a fact which he reminded her each time she berated him for coming home at one or two in the morning. She began spending her lonely evenings with her parents and Philomena, and did not notice the worried look on Paolo's face.

One Saturday, when he was not at the mill, Paolo visited Ugo at his warehouse with the excuse he might be interested in a furnace.

Ugo was happy to see his old friend and while he was busy extolling the marvels of the furnace, Paolo caught a glimpse of Frank coming into the office from outdoors with a pretty, young girl.

It was raining out and the two had shared a large black umbrella. As they entered the warehouse, Frank gave the girl a pat on her buttocks and when he spied Paolo, flushed uncomfortably. Before Frank could speak, Paolo said matter of factly. "I was asking Ugo about installing a new furnace for me."

"I didn't know you were interested, Papa Cook," said the embarrassed Frank.

"Perhaps you and Marie could come to dinner tonight and we could talk about it," said Paolo, ignoring the young girl who stood by unabashed by the proceedings of the last few minutes.

With that, Paolo thanked Ugo and went out the door hastily followed by an apologetic Frank. Paolo turned slowly, looking sternly on his flustered son-in-law and spoke with an authoritative voice. "I never judge any man until I have all the facts, but I expect my sons to be honest and loyal. I expect the same of you." With that he turned and left an unhappy Frank, standing in the rain, getting his new suit soaked.

That evening a very quiet Frank escorted his wife to dinner with her parents. Marie was happy with her husband's sudden attention and her face was all aglow when Paolo opened the door. During the balance of her pregnancy, Frank arrived home early each evening to an overjoyed wife. In June 1903, Marie gave birth to a bouncing baby boy, Frank Jr.; the proud father was delighted with his new son.

Paolo never mentioned the incident and was happy to see a glowing Marie with the joys of motherhood, a phenomenon observed by Frank also.

CHAPTER 29

*M*ost historians trace the beginning of the oil industry on a large scale to 1859. In the beginning, an old steam engine was used to power the drill to pump oil from the ground. Soon wells began to produce oil, and within three years, so much oil was produced that the price dropped from twenty dollars a barrel to ten cents.

By the early 1860's, the oil boom had transformed Pennsylvania and Ohio. Forests of wooden derricks covered the hills. Thousands of prospectors crowded into the small new boomtowns. Railroads built branch lines to the fields and began to haul oil throughout the eastern cities. Annual oil production in the United States rose from 2,000 barrels in 1859 to 64,000 by 1900.

Success stories such as the founding of the Ohio Oil Company in the oil fields of Findlay encompassed the likes of rough necks, storekeepers, bankers and men who were not afraid to take risks. It was into this great endeavor George and Joseph, ever inseparable, plunged eagerly. They found work in the oil fields and loved the atmosphere of rough and foolhardy men. This suited their adventurous hearts, especially the gambling instincts of the prospectors who were called "wildcatters." Fortunes were made in the oil business overnight and lost just as easily with the turn of a card.

After a grueling day in the fields, George and Joseph frequented the Red Eye Saloon. Here they swapped outrageous tales, drank moderately, and flirted with women. They played poker like a religion. Joseph was a gregarious poker player unlike George who sat stone-faced opposite his opponents. His methods were unnerving and many a pot was lost to him because of his inscrutable face. On weekends their favorite nightspot was Myra's, a house at the end of town where young men were willing to part with their weekly pay for favors eagerly given by the young painted girls.

The following year the twins invested in land rich in oil; they were on their way to becoming wealthy and their flashing good looks had sparked much interest from the local madam, as they were frequent visitors to her house of ill repute.

Some time had elapsed since they had been home, so planning a surprise, Paolo gathered up Rosa and Philomena, promising them a little vacation, and boarded the train for Findlay. Their sons were unaware of this and needless to say the trip was a disappointment for on their arrival they had run into George and Joseph strutting down the main street of Findlay, slightly inebriated, each with a flashy girl on their arm.

Paolo vainly tried not to discuss the meeting, but Philomena could not understand their hasty retreat from her brothers and kept asking her parents when she could see them again. He took Rosa and his little daughter to a quiet restaurant hoping to soothe Rosa's feelings, but she barely touched her meal and was eager to return home.

A week later a box of chocolates and a bottle of cognac were received at the Cook residence. Rosa gave the chocolates to a neighbor and Paolo never opened the cognac. The twins attempted to console their parents, but knew it was a losing situation; their lifestyle was deeply ingrained in their lives.

The following week, after a grueling day at the oil fields the two bathed and put on clean, fresh shirts and trousers made from a new material called denim. They made a handsome pair with their dark eyes and hair. Joseph had grown a moustache, which gave him a swashbuckling appearance. They were tall and slender and walked with the arrogance of youth, pants tucked into new cowboy boots, which was the style in such country.

"Saturday night, Joe," George shouted to his twin. "I'm ready for a tussle with one of the gals, you going to see Dolly?"

"Yeah, I got her some fresh fruit, oranges from Florida," answered Joseph.

"Myra would like to pair you off with that new girl, what's her name?" George laughed.

"Just to get her dander up I think I'll buy Dolly a steak dinner tonight," Joseph smirked.

Myra Flowers met them at the door. She was a big buxom woman who ran her house with a firm hand. All of her girls had come to her voluntarily and Myra protected them. Men were not allowed to abuse any of the residents. She also insisted the girls have a physical every six months. She would not abide disease and when a girl was found to be infected, she was sent to a farm to recuperate. Doc Turner examined the girls periodically and tried to enlighten them on how to protect themselves against disease. Most of the girls had never been instructed in hygiene and some laughed at his attempts.

"You're wasting your time on those poor things," Myra said and shook her head.

"But, Myra, you should help them too," Doc Turner answered.

"I do enough for them, let them help themselves a little," Myra answered in a flat tone.

When she had been caught in a swindle and angrily found herself in financial straits, George and Joe had come to her rescue, paying off her debts. She was casually grateful and each month paid off a little of the debt.

The twins always managed to have a fair amount of money to gamble. One night three professional gamblers stopped at the Red Eye Saloon, looking for a poker game. News spread rapidly throughout the town.

"Let's say we meander over to the saloon and watch for a while." George suggested.

"Okay by me, brother, I want to see how those guys operate,"

Joe answered.

The twins did not sit in on the game; instead they were interested spectators, good-naturedly buying drinks for the players. All the while, the gambling methods were being watched closely by George and Joe. George thought he saw the dealer pull a card from the bottom of the deck. He said nothing, storing the covert move in his mind.

A choice deed of land, rich in oil, was bet and added to the pot. The crowd that had gathered around the poker table became hushed. Tension ran high as the prospector sat clutching his cards to his chest, perspiration pouring from beneath his battered hat. Too late, he realized the prize he foolishly gambled was the dream every oilman fantasized. He was no match for the professionals opposite him. As the old prospector watched the triumphant gambler eagerly scoop up the winnings, he pulled out a revolver.

"Sumna bitch! You cheated!" he screamed.

Gunfire was exchanged and the prospector lay mortally wounded, blood oozing from his mouth.

"You all saw him pull a gun on me!" the gambler called out.

"Yes, yes, he pulled a gun!" the crowd shouted in unison.

The sheriff came running into the saloon. He took down all the names of the witnesses. It was a true case of self defense and the gambler was not held; however, the sheriff warned the group to leave the following day. They were not welcome in Findlay.

But Joe was not anxious for the gamblers to depart. Turning to his brother he growled, "Come on Pal, you and I are going to get even with those bums. The head guy cheated, sure as hell."

"Let's not be too careless, they look pretty ugly to me," George warned.

"We can handle them," Joe assured his brother.

"Yeah, but they have guns, we haven't, "George answered worriedly.

"They wouldn't touch us, not with the warning the sheriff gave them," Joe replied with a hint of bravado on his voice. "You don't want me to go alone, do you?"

"I'm going if only to keep you out of trouble," George countered. He did not want to be a part of this escapade but did not want to desert his brother, risky as the situation was. It had always been thus, Joe taking all the chances and George standing back, a little envious of his twin's bravado. He hesitated momentarily, then followed his brother out the door.

Going to the hotel where the gamblers were staying, Joe invited them to a poker game to be held at Myra's. The three professionals eagerly sat down with Joe and George to what they presumed to be a no-contest game. Two hours later, Joe was the jubilant owner of the deed of land rich with oil. Hank Stubbins, the leader of the group, was livid with anger. He had been out-smarted by a brash, young yokel.

"What do you aim to do, Hank?" asked a companion named Slick.

"Get my property back, damn it!" rasped Hank.

"You ain't gonna play poker agin, are ya?" Slick asked.

"He's a mighty fine poker player," volunteered Rusty, the third companion.

"I'm not sure he didn't cheat. Did any of you fellas see any shenanigans?" Hank asked.

"If he cheated, he was awfully good. We could use someone like him on our team," replied Rusty.

"He's not part of my team," shot back Hank. "I got to figure out a way to get my property back."

"That ain't gonna be easy," Rusty said anxiously. "We got to be careful with that sheriff, he seemed to mean business."

"Those two guys are mighty friendly with Myra, let's pay her a visit," Hank grinned.

After an unsuccessful talk with Myra, and still mindful of the sheriff's orders to be gone by daylight, the three began searching the streets of Findlay.

"We gotta separate those two," volunteered Rusty, remembering the two brothers seemed to be stuck like glue.

"Let's go back to Myra's," suggested Hank. "We might be able to bribe one of the gals. I'm sure they know where they live."

This time they were overly pleasant to Myra and flashed a large roll of money. Myra first of all was a business woman and soon the three were in the company of her prettiest girls. Hank ordered champagne for everyone and produced a slender string of pearls to his companion, Dolly. Mellowed by the champagne and the gift of pearls, she soon became talkative.

"Do you get many regulars here, Dolly?" asked Hank.

"Oh, sure. It's the same crowd every Saturday night," she answered, sipping her third glass of champagne.

"Most of them live right here in town?"

"Yeah, lots of them live in shacks. The guys who are better off live in the rooming house down the street."

"I guess the twins live at the rooming house, they look pretty successful."

"Sure, they live there. We ain't allowed there. That snooty manager, Holmes, kicked us out," pouted Dolly.

"I wouldn't kick you out, sweetie. Which room is theirs?"

"The one at the end of the hall." Too late she realized she made a mistake.

Snatching the string of pearls from around Dolly's neck, Hank strode out of the room calling for his friends, Rusty and Slick.

Dolly was too frightened to tell Myra and hoping to warn the twins, ran out the back door and raced towards the rooming house.

"Sheriff Townes! Sheriff Townes!" she screamed.

"What's up, Dolly?" hollered the sheriff, reaching for his shot-gun.

"Those gamblers are going after the Cook twins," gasped Dolly. "Hurry please!"

"I knew those slickers were bad news," Sheriff Townes rasped through clenched teeth. The sheriff fired a warning shot into the air and called out, "Stop or I will shoot to kill!"

The three stopped in their tracks and were taken into custody with Sheriff Townes handcuffing them to the hitching post outside the hotel. He ran back to the rooming house and up the stairs to the twin's room. Joe lay with his head on George's lap, his life's blood creating an ever-widening circle on the bedroom floor.

"It's okay, Joe," choked George stroking his brother's hair from his eyes. "I'm here."

"We sure showed up those slickers, didn't we?" Joe whispered.

'We sure did. Don't talk now, I'm sending for a doctor."

But Joe closed his eyes and stopped breathing. The deed was still secure in George's hidden money pouch. It seemed to be burning into his soul as he clasped his twin's lifeless body to him, tears running down his face and onto his brother's handsome face. Carrying him to the bed, giant sobs racked his body. Never had he felt such heart-wrenching pain and despair.

Later, he sent a wireless to Paolo informing him of the terrible tragedy and that he was bringing Joe's body home by rail; he asked his parents to meet him at the depot. The scene upon his arrival, with the entire Cook family present, was filled with weeping. Rosa was inconsolable as she whispered to Paolo she had lost touch with her sons and somehow had failed them. Paolo comforted her. "No Rosa, they lived the life they wanted."

George remained with his parents, he had no desire to return to Findlay. He had put his carefree days and rough and tumble ways behind him. In the months that followed, his days were filled with sorrow and at night his pillow was wet with tears.

CHAPTER 30

*D*ominic was ordained Father Dominic Cook, a title he accepted with great humility. He was sent to St. Patrick's Parish on the south side of Youngstown as an assistant. After serving Mass at St. Patrick's on the Sunday of Philomena's First Communion, he hurried to his parent's home, resplendent in his new priest's vestments. He was greeted by a very happy Philomena. George was there, bearing gifts for his little sister, as well as Marie and Frank, with Frank, Jr. and their new daughter, Christina. Vincenzo arrived with a lovely new friend, Gloria Manning, on his arm. Her golden beauty did not go unnoticed.

"Is this serious, old man?" asked Frank as they were getting a glass of wine.

"It could be, Frank, but I'm not ready to make any commitment yet," answered Vincenzo, smiling.

"Better hang on to that one, she's a knockout." Frank admired Gloria from across the room.

"Down, boy, she's all mine," laughed Vincenzo.

Vincenzo could have had his choice of the many girls who pursued him, but Gloria, with her tall regal beauty, intrigued him. Unlike his brothers, he did not wish to change his name to the English version, he loved the romantic sound of his name and in his profession felt it was more in keeping with the role he had chosen as a designer of modern homes.

His career had just taken off. He had been accepted into the school of design sponsored by Louis H. Sullivan, the great Chicago architect, and had no desire to be tied down. Gloria was fun and a good sport; he loved taking her to restaurants where everyone turned their heads when she walked by. He knew nothing of her background and it mattered little to him, he loved her company.

Several months passed since Philomena's communion celebration. Vincenzo had been hard at work and had seen Gloria only twice and now he sorely missed her. His designs at the new school had met with great approval and he was honored when he was chosen to attend a showing of the works of some of the country's leading architects to be held in Cleveland.

Obtaining permission to bring a guest to the showing, Vincenzo was eager to call upon Gloria and ask her to accompany him to Cleveland. Summoning a carriage, he hastened to her home, a box of candy in one hand and a bouquet of flowers in the other.

Her father, quite an elderly man, answered the door and stood blinking at Vincenzo, a harried look on his face.

"Good evening, Mr. Manning, remember me? I'm Vincenzo Cook. Is Gloria at home?"

The old man did not move, nor did he speak, as if in a daze.

"Mr. Manning, sir," said the perplexed Vinenzo. "Is something wrong? Is Gloria here?"

"Gloria is gone," whispered the old man, who seemed to be in great distress as he spoke.

"Where did she go?" asked Vincenzo, alarmed at Mr. Manning's state.

"She just up and left with that man, took all her clothes."

"But where did she go, and what man?" Vincenzo asked, and he began looking about the house, not completely comprehending the situation.

Mr. Manning had been a widower for ten years. Gloria was his only child and a headstrong one at that. They had many clashes over the years with Gloria getting her own way. As she grew older she came and went as she pleased, much to his disapproval. She had blossomed into a great beauty and was forever begging money from him to buy expensive gowns. He had an inheritance from his father, but his resources had dwindled over the years with Gloria making such demands. There had been harsh words the night before, she had threatened to leave, "with a man, any man," had been her exact words.

Vincenzo became alarmed as the old man began to weep, sinking down on the divan and clutching for air. Vincenzo ran into the street and hailing a carriage, entreated the driver to find a doctor as the man inside was in need of medical attention. Going back into the house, he sat beside the stricken man until a doctor arrived. The prognosis was dire, Mr. Manning had suffered a stroke.

Since no relatives were known to live in the immediate area, Vincenzo made arrangements that Mr. Manning should be moved to a rest home. In the meantime, he planned on trying to locate Gloria. He hired a lawyer who began a futile search; Gloria had completely disappeared.

In the meantime, things were not going well at the Massini home. Frank returned home one day with a swollen face and bloodied clothes and told a frightened Marie that he had been attacked and robbed by a band of men. He remained at home for several days, as fear pervaded his entire being. Marie was greatly puzzled and sought the advice of her father.

Having been through a similar experience in his youth, he tried to reassure Marie that Frank would be all right. Frank jumped every time someone knocked at the door and would not return to work. Ugo Massini was very concerned, especially since Frank's sales record had begun to slip and he had a poor showing for that month. Frank would not venture away from home at night and sat by the fire staring into the embers.

A secret society, called the Black Hand, organized for acts of terrorism and blackmail had infiltrated into Youngstown, Cleveland and Findlay, Ohio. The society was greatly feared especially by business men who were forced to pay protection monies for the safety of their enterprise and family. Frank had foolishly begun to gamble with members of the Cosa Nostra family introduced to him by his cousin, Jimmie Massini, a fast talking, flashy con man.

When Frank could not make good his gambling debts, his own cousin Jimmie had arranged the beating, hoping Frank had learned his lesson. But this did not wipe out the debt and Frank was terrified restitution would be brought on his family by the Black Hand. Finally in desperation he sought help from his uncle Ugo, who upon learning of his nephew's foolishness, refused help. He now had only one alternative and that was to beg money from his father-in-law, Paolo.

Paolo had heard of the Black Hand from workers at the mill who had stumbled into the same trap as Frank. Knowing the menace of the society, he gave Frank the money to pay off his debt with his sacred promise that his gambling days were over.

Frank, in the meantime, left his position with the Holland Furnace Company and joined the ranks of laborers at the mill, much to Marie's dismay. Their finances had never been at such a low and Marie begged to be permitted to go back to work in one of the many factories that had sprung up in Youngstown. Frank angrily turned on her, striking her for he first time in their marriage. Marie was heart-broken but never revealed Frank's treatment to her parents.

Meanwhile, trouble had been brewing in the mills. A steel strike at the Brier Hill Mill, beginning two days before Christmas, had idled fifteen thousand men. The men were demanding higher wages and an eight hour day. The scene was one of riot, death and destruction. Paolo never left the mill, eating and sleeping in his tiny office, in a brave attempt to appease the workers and try to find a solution for both management and workers.

Father Cook made an appearance, asking rioters to return to their homes and stop the bloodshed, but he was stoned by young men who had been his classmates at school. "Go hide behind your collar, Father. You don't belong here with working men," they taunted him.

"My father is a working man like you, why do you turn against him?" Dominic shouted, wiping blood from his forehead.

"He went over to their side, he's forgotten what it's like to work for pennies."

"You're wrong, he's one of you and will always be." But his words were in vain as they drove him off; he was ashamed he could not help his father in time of crisis.

Frank's anger festered inside him and soon became his entire being. He was unhappy with his home life and was filled with shame over his abuse of Marie. Hatred for his cousin Jimmie for having him beaten still rankled in his heart. He had become one of the rioters at the mill and, when the police had been brought in, he was in the middle of a bloody fight and was mortally wounded.

When Frank's body was brought home Marie wept uncontrollably. The Massini family held her responsible for Frank's death, saying she had not been a good wife, forcing him to belittle himself by working in the mill, he a college student. Paolo broke all ties with the Massinis, so angered was he over the treatment Marie had suffered.

Marie went to work in a munitions factory, refusing help from Rosa and Paolo, a matter of pride for her. Rosa insisted on caring for Frank Jr. and Christina; it was the least she could do.

CHAPTER 31

*I*n 1876 Alexander Graham Bell invented the telephone and the Bell Telephone Company was founded the next year. The general populous were leery of this new marvel and it wasn't until the early 1900's that telephones were installed in many private homes. Paolo decided it was time the Cook family should have this new invention, and upon its installation, they all stood around wondering whom to call. Their very first phone call was to City Hall inquiring about land tax tables.

Never having spoken on a telephone before there was great shouting into the mouthpiece and gesturing of hands by Paolo. In time, the proper procedure was acquired and a great deal of conversation was carried on over the new "voice box." It was several weeks before a timid Rosa gathered up enough courage to whisper into the mouthpiece. When a voice answered in the earphone, she dropped the magical instrument and ran for Paolo. What a gay time they had taking turns speaking with friends.

Winter came early that year, the lakes were frozen over and heavy snow fell every day, locking everyone indoors. Marie, Frank Jr. and Christina, spent a great deal of time with her parents in the big house next door. Rosa loved having the grandchildren, they brightened her life and for the time being helped her forget her sorrow.

George (the children called him Uncle G) delighted in little Christina, who made it quite clear to the family that he was her favorite uncle. He played games with her and read story books, sitting by the fire with her on his lap. She had inherited Paolo's blue eyes and George told Marie he was in her power when she turned her big eyes on him. Marie was grateful to her brother for his attention to her children. Frank. Jr. loved to spend hours with Paolo in the basement helping his grandpa sand a bookcase he was building for Rosa. Paolo would tell his little grandson stories of his life in Italy, the trip across the water to America and his job at the mill, promising to take the boy to the mill to see the giant furnaces.

The strike at the Brier Hill Mill had been reconciled with both worker and management satisfied with the results. Paolo was held in great esteem and respect for the part he played in the final outcome. His relationship with the workers over the years was greatly admired by all.

Henry Ford had founded the Ford Motor Company in 1903 and produced the first legendary Model T in 1908. Vincenzo bought one of the first Model T's and proudly drove it home that March. He had been working for Frank Lloyd Wright, one of the finest architects of the country, who had set up a studio in Oak Park, Illinois. One of the brightest stars of Adler & Sullivan Architects, Wright was accepting commissions on his own.

During the following years, Wright built his revolutionary "Prairie Houses," characterized by low-slung roof planes, ribbon windows, and terraces that extended the house into the landscape. On his trips home, Vincenzo raved over Wright's theory of "organic architecture" according to which buildings should blend naturally with their surroundings. Vincenzo learned of open planning by eliminating confining walls in buildings and creating dynamic interiors.

Vincenzo was at the height of his career, but with the loss of Frank and Joe felt he was not doing his part in the war effort. George had been talking about joining the army which made Vincenzo even more determined to do likewise. Rosa and Paolo were greatly distressed, they were fearful of more tragedy befalling the Cook family.

George was restless, having worked at odd jobs in Youngstown, never seeming to find his proper place in life. He had no romantic attachments, albeit many young women would gladly have surrendered to his charms. One evening after dinner, in a private conversation with Paolo and Rosa, George revealed he had signed up for the National Guard, and would be leaving the following week. Rosa and Paolo knew their son was unhappy and if this was his decision, they would honor it.

"I have a gift for you, Papa," said the young man, handing a legal document to Paolo.

"What is it, son?"

"It is a deed to my property in Findlay, made out in both your names. I'm almost certain there's oil on the land, but I don't have what it takes to drill for it. If you hold the deed long enough, I'm sure Standard Oil will want to buy it."

"But George, why don't you keep it for yourself?" said Rosa in amazement.

"I want you and Papa to have it, Mama," he answered. "If I ever am in need, you can divide the profits with me." He said it with such finality in his voice that it was agreed they would accept it on the condition half was his.

CHAPTER 32

The camaraderie of military life was a balm to George's aching heart; he and Joe had been so close all their lives. His commanding officer was a mean taskmaster, however, marching them twenty-five miles a day and making pontoon bridges in record time. George learned horsemanship and the use of explosives, and he learned to become a top-notch marksman. But would not indulge in Saturday night poker games.

On April 6, 1917, President Wilson signed the declaration of war against Germany, proclaiming, "The world must be safe for democracy." When he returned to the White House he was heard to say, "My message was one of death for young men. How odd it seems to applaud that." And he put his head in his hands and wept.

The first big decision of the war was to induct young men into the Army by lottery. The Selective Service Act was presented to the people and was passed by Congress on May 18, 1917. Next came the question, should the National Guard units fight? Which state's National Guard troops should be sent to France first? Parents in the designated states protested their boys were being marked for early sacrifice, yet on the other hand, guardsman in other states resented not being given first chance at the Germans.

German and French troops were dug in along a meandering line of fortified trenches, beginning at the North Sea and ending 466 miles away on the Swiss border. This was known as "no man's land" and the men crouched in the trenches as bullets cracked and shells flew by overhead. On June 25, 1917 the first U.S. troops began to arrive in France, forming the American Expeditionary Force. The American units did not enter the trenches until October; their presence was a much-needed boost to Allied morale.

Colonel Douglas MacArthur, the new division's Chief of Staff (and ultimately its commander) remarked that, "The 42nd Division stretches like a rainbow from one end of America to the other." It was called the Rainbow Division and George became a Sergeant in this historic unit. One of the first American divisions to reach the battlefields of the Western Front in November 1917, the Rainbow Division first saw action fighting alongside the French in February 1918.

The yellow poplar trees surrounding the forest once held singing birds, now their voices were stilled. Young men learned the sounds of gunfire and were able to detect what type was coming towards them, and their lives depended on how quickly they were able to dodge machine gun fire. It is said of the American soldier he had nerve and was so young and brash that he didn't know victory was nowhere in sight. The Rainbow stemmed the advance and launched counter attacks. Several days later, after heavy fighting, the Rainbow was relieved and the exhausted men rested for a few days.

Sergeant George Cook lay back upon his bunk dreaming of home. He had been gassed by the Germans and had lost so much weight the trousers of his uniform were held up by a belt that almost wound around him twice.

He lay on his side writing a letter to Marie. What a sweet sister she had always been. She wrote cheerful letters filled with all the news from home. He had searched for a girl like Marie, one who could be kind and loving. His mother had always told him he looked in the wrong places. "You can't find a good girl in brothels, son. Try church for a change." This remark always brought a smile to his face. So like Mama.

He had hated his brother-in-law, Frank, for his treatment of Marie. She deserved so much better. She had been a good wife and a wonderful mother to Frank, Jr. and Christina. Ah,

Christina! The light of his life with those big, blue eyes so like Papa's. He had showered her with gifts when he was stateside. Her tiny arms winding about his neck and her sweet mouth kissing his face lingered in his thoughts.

With death all around him, he knew how precious each life was and he was filled with tender memories of his formative years with the family. George called to mind how his father walked to the mill six days of the week through rain and snow and walked home each night weary and exhausted. And there would be Mama waiting at the window, with a smile lighting her face as he appeared at the door. He could never figure out Dominic, with his quiet, pious ways. Old Dom had never approved of him. He and Joe were "wild" Dom would say. I guess we were in a way, but at least we enjoyed life.

The boy in the next bunk reminded him of Joe with his dark, curly hair and brown eyes. He was barely nineteen years old and had hardly begun to live. "Hey, Sarge, what's the first thing you're going to do when we get back home?" he asked.

"Lay in a hot tub drinking a bottle of whiskey, then later eat a big plate of my mom's spaghetti," was George's reply.

"Sounds good to me. Where are you from, Sarge?"

"Youngstown, Ohio."

"I'm from Boise, Idaho. Sure miss my folks," was the choked reply. "Think we'll make it back home, Sarge?"

"Sure, kid, don't you know the Rainbow leads a charmed life?"

The division was ordered back into battle and the following week, Sergeant George Cook's body lay on a bloody wheat field in France thousands of miles from home. Private First Class Jimmie Burke gathered up Sergeant Cook's gear. When he spotted the small picture of the blue-eyed Christina he knelt beside his bunk and wept.

News of George's death hung like a black cloud over the Cook home. Paolo and Rosa both became extremely depressed.

Now with Vincenzo also in the army, Paolo decided to retire from the mill. He spent his days painting the house, and replacing all the screens on the windows and doors. His favorite time, however, was digging in the earth. It brought back memories of his youth and of that time when he was only a boy farmer. Lately, his thoughts wandered back over those years.

He remembered only dimly the faces of his parents and his brothers and sister and how terrified he had been finding himself all alone in a cold world. He remembered fondly the good farmer, Luigi Romano, who had been like a father to him. His life began anew when he met Rosa. His love for her had grown with each passing year. Not only had she given him eight beautiful children, but she had been his helpmate, partner and friend.

Paolo and Rosa never missed going to Calvary Cemetery each Sunday to bring flowers to the graves of Lucia, Antonio, George, Joe, and Luigi. The grief they shared over the loss of those loved ones never left them and Paolo searched for the answers to life's tragedies; he was saddened when he failed. He had hoped someday to pass onto his children some legacy which would prove to them he had been a success in this life. He had given his family a good home and security, but sadly, he would have wished for more worldly goods to bequeath to them.

He need not have been distraught for his wife and children adored him. He was their strength, their balance wheel and assurance all was well in their world. His days were now precious, for the twilight of his years with Rosa brought a joyous shared devotion and complete fulfillment.

Books had always been Rosa's passion and now she was in love. Having found the works of such great writers as Elizabeth Barrett Browning, Robert Louis Stevenson and Walt Whitman, it seemed there was not enough hours in the day to indulge in her pleasure.

"My life could never be long enough to read all the books I want," she would lament. She had bought a slim volume of

Elizabeth Barrett Browning's sonnets and each night after dinner, she and Paolo sat by the fire and she read aloud the most beautiful of Browning's poems: *"How do I love thee...let me count the ways."* Paolo would light his pipe, sit back in his easy chair and listen to Rosa's voice, still as sweet and melodic as when she was a young girl reading aloud for Contessa Juliana de Salvatore.

CHAPTER 33

*B*ecause Vincenzo had completed a JROTC program along with his four-year college degree, he joined the army as a Second Lieutenant and was sent to Fort Leavenworth for training. It was not to his liking. This was a rough, tough group of men, but he learned to accept his role as officer and in November, he was sent overseas.

Vincenzo had been in the midst of the fighting. He had lost track of time and only knew he had not slept for forty-eight hours. He was covered with mud, his troop had slogged through the wet forest, hungry and dog-tired. A relief troop came none too soon and the weary men were able to fall back and get some much needed rest.

Upon arrival at the camp headquarters, Vincenzo reported to his superiors, then finding his way back to his tent, fell upon his bunk and without removing his filthy clothes, slept. He was awakened after six hours by an orderly with orders to report to General Howes.

He bathed, shaved, donned a clean uniform, and set out to report to the General. A Salvation Army truck had pulled up and he saw a woman handing out hot coffee and doughnuts to the enlisted men. Vincenzo caught only a glimpse of the golden hair, a heavy uniform concealed the rest. Vincenzo continued his walk to the General's quarters, intuitively stopped and walked in the direction of the truck.

Peering inside he saw the golden beauty face to face. "Gloria?" he asked incredulously.

"Vinnie!" was the equally amazed reply.

Later that night as Gloria sat curled up on Vincenzo's bunk, he learned of her strange disappearance. Frustrated with the smallness of Youngstown and her continual lack of money, Gloria had fallen victim to the age-old tale of fame spun by a master of the game. Her beauty would grace the movies, he told her; his world seemed filled with glamour and wealth. He took her to expensive restaurants and showered her with gifts. They went to Hollywood aboard the luxurious Chief railroad car where she had her own private suite. She was dazzled and the attention went to her head like strong wine.

When they arrived in Hollywood, his true intentions came to the front. He attempted to lure her into a brothel frequented by famous directors and wealthy producers. But Gloria, disillusioned, did not succumb. Alone and without funds, she turned to the Salvation Army who took her in. Her work with those good souls mended her shattered pride. She learned to drive a truck and when war was declared, she volunteered for overseas duty.

"And now here we are, Vinnie, in this God-forsaken place. Lord knows I never expected to see you here, "she sighed as she inhaled the cold night air. "Oh, and Vinnie, I want to thank you for all the many kindnesses to my father. He was able to die in dignity because of you. I will always be grateful."

"I searched for you, Gloria," he breathed softly, then taking her in his arms, kissed her waiting lips. The ugliness of the war, the smell of death, and the urgency of the moment were all forgotten as they made love. First wildly, then tenderly.

The next day his troop was ordered to the front once more and as they bid farewell he whispered, "Don't disappear again, sweetheart. Wait for me."

"I will Vinnie, I promise."

The next months were a living hell as he and his men fought desperately against almost unsurmountable odds. Every man was a hero, each one shielding the other, and the feeling was they were all brothers clinging together in the face of a terrible enemy.

Where is George, he wondered as he crouched in the trenches, not knowing of his brother's death. Send him home safely to Mama and Papa, he prayed. He thought he heard his mother singing, and looking up caught sight of a flaming red ball coming towards him, then all was darkness.

He awoke days later and found himself in a hospital. A nurse was bending over him, stethoscope in hand. Straightening up she spoke in a cheerful voice, "Well, it's about time you woke up. Had me worried for a bit."

"Where am I?" asked Vincenzo as he tried to sit up but fell back in pain.

"Whoa there, Captain. You've been wounded in more than one place."

"But I'm Lieutenant Cook, nurse," gasped Vincenzo as he lay upon his pillows.

"Not anymore, you've been promoted, Sir," answered the smiling nurse. "And to answer your first question, a beautiful blonde lady left this letter for you." Reaching into her pocket she brought out an envelope.

Dear Vinnie: I stayed as long as I was permitted, until I was re-assured you will be alright and will return home soon. I have been ordered back to the States where I and our expected child will be waiting for you. I love you. Gloria.

Vincenzo lay back on his pillows, face wreathed in smiles. He longed for his discharge but it would be months before he was well enough to travel. He had lost his right foot and was fitted with a prosthesis that was clumsy and awkward. "It's my damn kicking foot," he told the doctor. Hell, who needs football any more, he thought, and swore when he stumbled and fell.

CHAPTER 34

*P*aolo had begun a journey into pain and tried vainly to keep Rosa from detecting it. One night, however, she was greatly alarmed when he awoke crying out.

"Paolo, what's wrong?" There was terror in her voice as she wrapped her arms about him.

"It's nothing, Rosa go back to sleep."

"Tomorrow we go see Dr. Montani," Rosa said firmly.

But the examination proved to be a blow as they learned a cancer was growing in Paolo's stomach. Rosa's heart was filled with anguish as she watched the strong body weaken over the next few weeks, so much that he could barely rise up in bed. Her tears wet her pillow each night as she lay beside him. She prayed Vincenzo would return home before it was too late.

It was Sunday morning, April 3, 1918 and when Rosa arose the sun was shining in the window so brightly that she proceeded to draw the blinds halfway. Paolo spoke softly, "Let me see the sun, Rosa, this may be the last time."

Glancing quickly and with panic in her heart, she rushed to his bedside.

"Oh, Paolo, don't leave me!" she entreated.

"I must go now, it's time. I love you, my beautiful Rose."

He let out a long sigh, then quickly sat up in bed, staring off into space, his blue eyes flooded with tears and cried out, "Papa!" A faint smile crossed his face. He sank back down on the bed and then the gallant heart stopped beating.

Vincenzo returned home two days later and sat weeping beside his father's body that had been laid out in a polished wooden casket in the parlor. Rosa clung to him in her sorrow, yet there was joyful relief that her son had returned from the war.

After the funeral, when everyone had gone, Rosa sat in their bedroom alone. Her pain and sense of loss overwhelmed her. She sat rocking in the chair Paolo had bought her many years ago, tears streaming down her face. She was remembering all the joys and sorrows of her life. Could anyone have had a better life? Paolo had never spoken a harsh word to her in all their years of marriage. He professed his love for her in so many ways.

Each night at bedtime, he would lean over and say, "I love you, Rosa." How she missed that now and how she missed his strong arms about her. His body and love had been a shield protecting her and now a terrible sense of abandonment enveloped her. I must be strong for my children, she determined. Philomena needs me and Vincenzo has told me I will have a new grandchild soon.

Vincenzo and Gloria were quietly married. He had wanted to be married in St. Joseph's Church where he had been baptized, and made his First Communion. But Gloria, being a Mormon, would not hear of it. So they compromised and were married by a Justice of the Peace.

Rosa was appalled and extremely saddened by this turn of events, but she would not interfere. The ceremony was a brief affair with only Rosa and Marie present. However, Rosa had prepared a late buffet for the young couple on their return home from the courthouse. Philomena turned on all the lights in the dining room when she heard them coming in the front door and ran to hug her brother and Gloria.

When Vincenzo's son was born, Gloria won Rosa's heart forever when she named the baby boy Paul Vincent Cook. How proud Paolo would have been! Dominic was horrified at his brother's indiscretion and forbade Philomena to have anything to do with Gloria, fearful she would be a bad influence on his young sister. But in her wisdom, Rosa knew her young daughter was strong in her own moral convictions and was pleased when Philomena greeted her new sister-in-law with love and warmth.

But a serious rift developed between Vincenzo and Dominic as the latter held Gloria in great contempt and refused to even to speak to her. Father Dominic could not understand his mother allowing such a sinful woman in their home and treating her as though she had never committed the adulterous act of which she was surely guilty. Gloria tried to win approval by allowing Paul to be baptized, but on the day of the christening, Father Dominic had spurned Gloria so that it brought tears to her eyes.

Clutching Father Dominic by his clerical collar, Vincenzo hissed in his face, "Listen, you sanctimonious bastard, that's my wife and the mother of my son. You treat her with respect!"

"Never! She's nothing but a whore!"

Hearing such words from his brother, Vincenzo struck him a blow that sent him flying into the divan.

Rosa came running out of the room where she had placed baby Paul's crib, crying out, "Boy's! What has gotten into you two? I will have no fighting!"

Rosa was dismayed when she learned of Father Dominic's actions and asked him to apologize to Gloria and Vincenzo, and when he would not, ordered him to leave. Dominic vowed he would never again return to his mother's house.

Part Four:
Generations

CHAPTER 35

Damien

As was the custom in Italy in 1872, the second eldest son stood next in line to inherit what remained of his brother's wealth. Upon arriving at Castello del Sole, Pasquale de Salvatore made haste to remove whatever vestige of Elena that he could, without touching the section set aside by law as Elena's park. Gone were the lovely rooms and rose gardens, replaced with heavy ornate furniture and a stone courtyard.

When Pasquale entered his mother's quarters, his eyes fell upon Damien asleep in his crib. Contessa Juliana de Salvatore overheard Pasquale plotting with his man-servant to kidnap the child and give him over to a band of gypsies.

At Elena's death, the Contessa had the good sense to hire an investigator to seek the whereabouts of Leo Palumbo, Damien's true father. She contacted her uncle, Archbishop Scolesi, and told him of Pasquale's ugly plot. The Archbishop sent an envoy to help. Together they gathered up Damien and all the money Juliana had with her to set off for a home long ago bequeathed to the Archbishop in the seaside city of Bari in the region of Apulia. The envoy returned to the castle and gathered up from their hiding place all the jewels Juliana had hidden.

Pasquale was furious when he discovered she had left and swore she could never return. Juliana took her cook and good friend, Josephina. Together they lived twelve years in the house in Bari where Damien had a happy childhood. Part of Juliana's diligent preparation for Damien's certain future in America was to teach him English and a tutor had been hired for that purpose.

In Damien's twelfth year, Juliana realized her time on earth was coming to an end. She contacted Archbishop Scolesi and told him of her plight. The Archbishop contacted Leo, whom he discovered lived in grand style in Cleveland, Ohio, and told him he would be sending his son to America to live with him. Knowing that Damien would be provided for by his father, Contessa de Salvatore donated what remained of her vastly dwindled wealth and jewels to the St. Anthony's orphanage for girls in Bari.

Damien grieved Juliana's passing, she had been a devoted *nonna* to him. He wandered alone along the busy streets of Bari and wondered if he would see her again in heaven one day. When he learned he would be going to America on a ship to live with his father, he was elated. The Archbishop's envoy, Ramon, gathered up Damien with his possessions and accompanied him across the sea.

Twelve days later after a relatively calm voyage, Damien and Ramon disembarked in New York City, went through immigration at Castle Garden, and finally boarded a train for the overnight trip to Cleveland.

When they arrived at the train station, a fine black carriage with matching horses was waiting to take them the last few miles to the Palumbo estate. Damien could only sit in complete wonder and surprise at its grandeur. Approaching the mansion along the road, huge, flowering trees were planted on each side and crimson bougainvillea covered the fences. Green ivy grew up the outside walls and pink and white roses covered a wrought-iron trellis.

An attendant who had been waiting for their arrival escorted Damien and Ramon through double doors of carved oak into a circular foyer twenty-feet high. There were paintings everywhere, dozens of different scenes: Seascapes, mountains, sea-faring men, children and old women. He came upon many portraits of a beautiful young woman, with long blonde hair falling over her shoulder. Her eyes were a magnificent, glowing blue. He gasped in surprise, she looked a lot like himself. Damien was mesmerized, a voice behind him broke the spell.

"Well, well, we finally meet! Your name is Damien, is it not?" A tall, blond man with suntanned visage spoke in Italian and extended his hand in a formal welcome.

"*Si, Signore. Io sono Damien*," he blurted.

"We have hired a tutor for you so you will become an American. His name is Mr. Greco and he will take care of you." With that, Leo Palumbo turned and left the room.

Damien stood looking at the closed door in utter disbelief and disappointment; his father had been so distant and cold. "Doesn't he care that I am his son?" Tears came to his eyes. Suddenly, from another doorway in the cavernous hall emerged a rotund man with a large moustache, a mouthful of white teeth and curly white hair.

Calling out to Damien, he extended his hand in greeting. "Master Damien, I am so glad to make your acquaintance. I am so sorry I am late, but we will work together, you and I, to make you an American." Damien wiped the tears from his eyes with the back of his hand. Smiling, he repeated the gesture with an outstretched hand.

"Come, come, Damien. Come to my house and meet my wife, she has prepared a dinner for us."

Mrs. Greco was equally rotund matching her husband's figure; she was jovial and hugged Damien as though he were a member of the family. The meal was just what Damien needed, different tasting, not the same as his *nonna*, but so good he asked for more.

From then on, Damien lived with the Mr. and Mrs. Greco and spent weekends at his father's house, mostly alone except for the caretakers and gardeners. Leo sent a stipend every month to the Grecos for his keep, relieved he could avoid responsibility for his son and happy to be with his monied friends.

Damien was an excellent student, eager for the time he could enter public school; his English would have to be much improved, however, to be accepted, as this was the policy at the time. If a child did not speak well enough, they were sent home.

After he passed the written and spoken examination, he was admitted into public school where his accomplishments were outstanding. Damien's integration into American life was so rapid, Mr. and Mrs. Greco could not help but be amazed and proud.

Mr. Greco took Damien to baseball and football games, and he delighted in the child's enthusiasm as the young boy hollered and cheered, just as the other young men. Mr. Greco learned Damien practiced kicking a football in a field near his father's home and hoped someday to be a player.

The time passed swiftly, and now in the September, he would be entering the 11th grade. On the first day at Cleveland High School, meeting the junior class of young men and women, he was grudgingly accepted by the male students, who were impressed with the well-dressed Damien, who confidently shook hands with them, smiling all the while. Because his father had become a naturalized citizen, Damien was also, and he carried himself like a proud U.S. citizen. The young girls of his class were wide-eyed with interest in the tall, blond man with the startling blue eyes, and they loved his slight accent.

Damien was particularly anxious to meet the football coach, Brett Johnson, and rather formally, asked the principal if he would arrange a meeting. The principal was curious at the manner of request until Damien explained he wanted to try out for the team. He agreed and took Damien out to the field to meet Coach Bret Johnson.

"Brett," he called out. "I have someone who wants to meet you and try out for the team. This is Damien Palumbo."

A middle-aged man wearing a school jacket and chewing on a wad of gum, came forward. He noticed at once that the young man walking toward him was well-built and strong. Extending his hand in greeting, Coach Johnson asked, "So, Damien, you want to try out for the team?"

"Yes, sir."

"Can you kick a football, Damien?"

"Yes, sir, I sure can."

"Well, let's see how you do. Go over to the bin, pick out a football and come with me to the field."

Damien did as he was told and returned to where Coach was standing patiently, thinking the young man probably could not kick far. Damien took off his jacket, walked to where Coach stood, assumed the proper stance, and drop-kicked the football to the very end of the field. Running down field, he retrieved the ball and kicked it all the way back where Coach stood.

Coach Johnson opened his mouth, dropped the wad of gum and exclaimed, "How did you learn to do that?"

"I practice every week-end in the field next to my father's house." Damien smiled. His hard work and diligence had paid off!

"Come on, lad, let's meet the other guys and get you suited up." He introduced Damien to the team, many of whom had seen the kicking demonstration, and were eager for the new teammate. Needless to say, Cleveland High School went undefeated that year and the next. The crowds were so large, the school council added more seats to the bleachers.

But after graduation, Damien did not want to play football in college. He wanted to devote all his time to studying for a teaching degree, like Mr. Greco, who was so elated at the young man's choice of profession. Mr. Greco helped Damien apply for and receive a scholarship that would earn him a degree in education. For the next four years, he worked diligently; the subject he chose was mathematics, specifically algebra.

CHAPTER 36

*L*eo Palumbo's life had changed dramatically. He had become so arthritic he could no longer paint, therefore, it was imperative for him to sell some of the large portion of his paintings that he still possessed. He had already sold his mansion and moved to Youngstown, a city that was not comparable in size to Cleveland.

He needed to live a quieter life than his friends, he could no longer afford to associate with them and, most of all, he was not well. He still provided the monthly stipend to Damien, who knew nothing of his father's failing health. However, one day Mr. Greco received a letter from Leo telling him he needed Damien to come to Youngstown where he could be told the true circumstances of his birth, before it was too late.

Damien hurriedly packed his bags and set out for his father's home, all the while berating himself for being so unkind. His father never asked anything from him and now he needs me, he repeated over and over.

Arriving at the address given him, he was greatly surprised by the small house. With trepidation, he rang the doorbell, which was answered by a young man who spoke softly. "We have been expecting you, Damien. Come, I will take you to Mr. Palumbo."

Damien could not believe his eyes, there lying in bed with pillows propping him up was a shadow of the former man, his father, no longer the sun-drenched, handsome figure, holding out a shaking, crippled hand. "Ah, Damien. It is so good to see you again."

Damien grasped the arthritic hand and knelt on the floor beside Leo's bed. "Why didn't you send for me sooner? I would have come immediately," he cried.

"You have done well, Damien," Leo whispered. Then he reached for two small books lying at his feet. "I am at the end of the road and wanted to tell you about your true birth. I have a diary belonging to Elena, your mother, and another from Juliana." Handing the books to Damien, he began his story in a hushed voice.

The illegitimacy of his birth stunned Damien. Leo, in his youth, had been a free spirit, carelessly moving from romance to romance. Damien wondered if perhaps he had siblings in America, or maybe still in Italy. Leo did not think so, Damien was his only child. But for the remainder of his life, he would look for a brother or sister. He resented his father for keeping such a secret all these years. Why couldn't he have told him?

But now, looking at his father, he felt a deep pity. Leo was dying and his confession had given his sunken face a warm glow. Leo had made peace with his son and felt cleansed. Leo grasped Damien's hand and whispered, "Forgive me son, always remember I love you," and with that drew his last breath and was gone.

Damien lay his head upon his father's chest and wept. He wept for the young girl who was his mother and whose face shone down from so many of the paintings in the studio. He wept that he had never known her, then he wept for himself. Leo had left a legacy, not only in money but in a great collection of paintings, which he now packed carefully, crating and storing them in a large warehouse. He then went to Leo's studio for the purpose of meeting the young man who was the gallery manager.

Fred Peterson was surprised when Damien held out his hand in greeting, and saddened to learn that Leo Palumbo had died. For a moment Damien thought he saw a frightened look cross Fred's face as if he wondered whether, with Damien as the new owner, he would be asked to leave his position, which he did not want to do; he loved his job.

"Fred, I am not going to ask you to leave. I want only to tell you I will be elsewhere. I would like you to stay on in your present position. I ask that you continue to take the day's receipts to the bank for deposit in the Palumbo estate, as you have always done."

Fred Peterson was surprised at this turn of events and the simple request from Damien, but with great enthusiasm, promised him he would comply with his wishes and provide Damien with a complete report every month.

Having completed this task on his deceased father's behalf, Damien was now restless and at odds with himself. After the American entry into WWI in 1917, he enlisted in the Armed Forces as a lieutenant and was assigned the position of Quartermaster in charge of munitions, which were sent to the various posts and later to Europe. He was extremely proficient in his job. The amount of food, clothing and arms provided by the Americans was staggering. He was in charge of a great deal of the distribution and took this responsibility with his characteristic dedication and diligence.

Strangely enough, army life was an exhilarating change for Damien. He had escaped the drudgery of school and thrust himself whole-heartedly into his new job. His methodical disposition and attention to detail gained him the admiration of his commanding officer, Colonel Thomas E. Lewis.

Colonel Lewis had three unmarried daughters, ages seventeen, twenty-two, and thirty. Never wanting to play the role of match-maker, the Colonel nevertheless would have welcomed Damien as a son-in-law. His eldest daughter, Helen, had raised the younger girls after the death of his wife fifteen years before. She had put aside her own dreams and had shunned any romantic involvement in order to raise her sisters and make a home for her father. She was a slender woman with grey eyes and shining auburn hair that she wore piled high in a braided crown. Her handsome face could not disguise her cool demeanor. Suitors, initially eager, soon lost interest when confronted by her lack of enthusiasm and haughty ways.

Now Colonel Lewis had grand hopes for Helen and invited Damien to dinner. Helen was an excellent cook and she had prepared a sumptuous meal at her father's request. The younger girls, Rosemary and Marion, were smitten with Lieutenant Palumbo and kept up a merry dialogue with Damien. The event was an embarrassment for Helen, who after dinner, retreated to her room. Her father had made his plans so obvious.

In spite of Colonel Lewis's bungled efforts, Damien was attracted to Helen. He called upon her the following week and they enjoyed a leisurely lunch overlooking Hudson Bay. Helen was knowledgeable about the plight of the American Indian, having read about the massacre at Wounded Knee in 1890; she had begged her father to allow her to go to Washington D.C. and lobby on behalf of justice for Native Americans. But being a military man Colonel Lewis did not share his daughter's concerns and discouraged all mention of such matters.

Damien discovered Helen was a comfortable person to be with. He was lonely, and he found himself wanting to be in her company on week-ends. Sundays she devoted to her father, playing the role of the perfect daughter.

It was not long, however, when Damien became aware that Helen had a father fixation. When he suggested a trip to New York City for the two of them, Helen demurred, saying she could not leave her father alone on Sunday.

"But Helen, the girls will be here to look after him," he argued.

"You don't understand, he needs me," she stated, pursing her lips in finality.

Damien was angry. He came to the sad conclusion that any man married to Helen would always remain in the Colonel's shadow. His visits became fewer and fewer, until they ceased altogether.

On the morning of Monday, November 11, 1918 the State

Department announced that Germany had surrendered and signed an armistice stating that all fighting in the World War would cease. It is true the Allies could not have defeated the Central Powers without the aid of the United States. A whole generation of Europeans was maimed and faint with exhaustion when the United States sent into the battlefield two million brash and lusty men.

When peace was declared, Damien was ready to become a civilian again. Restless and lonely, he was eager to tie the ends of his life together, so traveling to Youngstown, he sought out the Cook family. With his muster-out pay from the army, and some money left to him by his father, he invested $1,700 in a new, four-door Studebaker Big Six, a real luxury for anyone. As he drove up the familiar street, he caught sight of some teen-aged boys tossing a football back and forth. The scene brought back many happy memories of his youth.

He stopped in front of the Cook home. One young boy of perhaps sixteen, called out, "Nobody's home."

"Do you know the Cook family?" Damien asked the young boy, who looked vaguely familiar.

"Sure, Rosa Cook is my Grandma," and then added in an admiring tone, "I sure like your car."

"Thank you. What's your name?" Damien wondered, could this be Marie's son?

"My name is Frank Massini. What's yours?"

"I'm Damien Palumbo. Do you like football?"

"I love it, but my mom won't let me play on the team," Frank answered with a trace of anger in his voice.

"What about your dad? What does he say?"

"My dad's dead. He wouldn't have cared anyhow. My Grandpa would have talked my mom into letting me play, but he died too."

Just then Rosa came around the corner, loaded down with grocery bags. Frank ran to her assistance, scolding her. "Grandma, why do you carry so many heavy bundles?"

Rosa caught sight of Damien, dropped the bags in Frankie's arms and rushed to greet him. "Damien! It's so good to see you," and with tears in her eyes, threw her arms around the smiling man.

Damien was touched by the warmth of her greeting and helping Frank with the groceries, proceeded into the house. He was filled with nostalgia as he looked about the familiar surroundings. Nothing has changed, he thought. We had such good times here.

"I see you've met my grandson, Frankie," said Rosa, as she hurried about in her customary manner, laying out plates on the dining room table.

"Yes, we've met. And how is Marie?"

"Marie is fine. She was working at the munitions factory, but now that the war is over, she has gone back to her secretarial job at Republic."

"I heard about Mr. Cook. I am so sorry."

For a moment, Rosa choked back a tiny sob and wiped away a tear. With anguish in her voice, she said, "We lost George and Joseph, too."

"Oh, no! I didn't know." Then added emotionally, "I lost my father a month ago."

Going over to Rosa, he put his arm about her and they wept together.

"I brought you a gift, Mrs. Cook. It's in the car."

He returned with a large painting, and setting it on the divan, turned to Rosa and said, "My father was an artist, you know. He always loved this particular painting. I thought you might like to have it. He told me it was done in an Italian garden that he loved."

And there before Rosa was the lovely courtyard, resplendent with Paolo's roses, the beautiful marble fountain and the aviary she had always admired. Falling to her knees before the lovely scene, Rosa cried out, "Paolo's roses!"

Damien was astonished and reached down for Rosa, "You've been there before, haven't you?" He realized this was a familiar place.

"Yes, I have. Paolo planted those roses," she answered, tears streaming down her face.

Damien was even more incredulous when he asked, "You knew my mother too?"

"I did. We spent many happy days sitting in the garden. She was a beautiful woman. May I tell you?"

"My father told me about my mother just before he died. You knew all the time?"

For the next hour, Rosa related the entire story and when she told him of Elena's death, the young man sat with his head in his hands.

How did Damien happen to come to Youngstown, Ohio from Bari, Italy and stranger still, how did his life become intertwined with the Cook family? Was it merely Fate, or are their cosmic forces that some say govern our lives? There is a theory, little known, that the unborn souls wait in heaven, choosing where they are to be born and to whom. Had Damien, while in Limbo, mapped out his life so he could become a part of the Cook family?

Calling to Frankie, Rosa ordered him to bring hammer and nail to hang the lovely painting. With the aid of Damien, it was hung over the fireplace, lighting up the entire room. Rosa stood as if transfixed before the lovely scene, drinking in all its beauty, her mind wandering back over the years, envisioning Paolo showing her his roses. This was the most precious gift she had ever received, and told Damien so. He was deeply moved he had been the bearer of such an instrument of joy.

"You will stay for dinner, Damien," Rosa insisted. "Marie will be happy to see you." She put on her apron and walked into the kitchen.

"I wouldn't miss one of your delicious meals, Mrs. Cook."

Just then, Frankie entered the dining room, followed by

Christina, a twelve-year old version of Marie, but with Paolo's blue eyes. "Oh, what a lovely painting," she exclaimed. "Where did it come from?"

"It's a gift from Damien," Rosa answered, smiling. "Christina, this is Damien Palumbo, a dear friend of the family. His father, Leo, was a very famous artist."

Christina shyly shook Damien's hand. "Do you know my mother?" she asked.

"Yes, she came to all the football games your Uncle George played," he answered. A cloud passed over her face at the mention of her Uncle G. She had mourned his death nearly as much as Rosa. He had been her favorite uncle and she remembered how sweet and kind he had been to her.

As children, she and Frankie loved being with their grandparents. The Cook home was always warm and full of love. Marie had become quiet and withdrawn, loving but in a world all her own. At bedtime, she listened to their prayers, gently kissed them, then spent the evenings reading alone in her room.

Frankie was more outgoing than Christina and paid no heed to Marie's quiet ways. He spent a great deal of time with his Uncle Vincenzo, who had set up a studio not far from the Cook home. Vincenzo's work fascinated the young boy and when Vincenzo went out on a surveying job, Frankie was invited to go along.

It was six o'clock when Marie came home from work. The room grew quiet as Damien and Marie came face to face.

"Hello, Marie," he said softly. "It's good to see you again."

The years melted away. Maria was again the eager sixteen-year-old girl and he the young algebra teacher and football coach. "Hello, Damien. It's good to see you, too."

"Come see the beautiful painting Damien gave Grandma," Christina said, kissing her mother.

Damien remembered the beautiful young girl in a faded bathrobe with an awful sock around her neck and black curls falling down her back. Marie remembered a tall, handsome man, wearing a white cable-knit sweater, laughing with her noisy brothers.

Suddenly, from far away. Marie heard her daughter calling out, "Mama, come see the painting."

"It's so beautiful," Marie sighed. As Marie stood before the painting, Rosa explained its location and the enormity of the co-incidence connected with it. "It was so good of you, Damien, to give it to Mama."

"Had I know its true significance, I would have begged my father to give it up years ago."

"Come, come, let's all sit down to dinner. Frankie will be happy to have a man around for a change," Rosa said laughing.

When supper had ended and the dishes cleared away, Damien spoke of his plans for the future. When he first arrived in Youngstown, he expected to go back to Cleveland. But now, finding Marie as a widow, he began to formulate a different plan for himself. Now he spoke. "I'll look up Vincenzo. I may want to set up a studio for my father's paintings. Then I'll see what turns up."

Damien glanced at Marie. She was smiling. He knew he had come back to Youngstown for good.

CHAPTER 37

Philomena

The women's rights movement began inconspicuously with five women who met for tea on July 9, 1848. Four of the women were Quakers, Lucretia Mott, her sister Martha Wright, Mary Ann McClintock and Jane Hunt. The fifth woman was Elizabeth Cady Stanton, the mother of seven children, who later was known as the founder of the women's rights movement.

Lucretia Mott was denied a seat with her husband at a slavery conference in London. It was here Lucretia and Elizabeth first met. They discussed women's rights and vowed to meet again to formulate a plan to do something about the issues. She appeared before every Congress from 1869 to 1906 to ask for passage of a constitutional amendment for suffrage.

After a 70-year battle, the 19th Amendment, which stated that "the rights of citizens of the United States to vote shall not be denied or abridged by the United States or by any State on account of sex," passed both houses of Congress, and in 1919 was sent to the states for ratification.

On August 18, 1920, Tennessee became the 36th state to ratify the amendment, giving it the two-thirds majority of state ratification necessary to make it the law of the land. Eight days later, the 19th Amendment took effect. Susan B. Anthony did not live to see the amendment enacted, as she died in 1906.

Philomena, with her independent manner, had become an active suffragette, co-ordinating marches down Federal Street and passing out handbills on her one day off from work. Imagine her joy when the amendment, which had been blocked for years, was approved by Congress and struggle ended quietly, August 26, 1920. She rushed home to give her mother the good news.

"Now we can go to the polls together, Mama. Isn't that exciting?" she shouted, grabbing Rosa by the waist and twirling her around.

"Philomena!" Rosa cried out breathlessly. "Save all that energy for a trip you and I have to take."

"A trip? Where? When do we leave?" asked Philomena gaily.

"I must talk with Vincenzo first. It's partly a business trip. I'll explain later."

Rosa had dreamed of going to Findlay with Paolo to sell the deeded land and present a handsome sum to Joseph upon his return home from the war. Sadly, laying aside her dreams, she now wished to establish a legacy she could pass on to her children. She sought out the advice of Vincenzo, explaining the deed Joseph had left her and Paolo.

"I would say you have a valuable parcel of land, Mama," Vincenzo said after reading the documents. "My advice to you is to sell the land to Standard Oil as soon as possible and enjoy the monies received. Would you like me to look into the matter for you?"

"No, I will take Philomena with me and deal with the matter myself," answered Rosa.

"Don't make any snap decisions. Tell them you will consider their offer," warned Vincenzo.

"I'll do just that, son. Thank you."

And so it was decided that a very eager Philomena would accompany Rosa to Findlay and meet with the official in charge of Standard Oil Company at that office. When the two women arrived in Findlay, they obtained a room at the only hotel in town. They planned on making this excursion a short vacation, combining business with pleasure.

Philomena had shed her quiet ways and had developed a dynamic personality. "She met life head on," Vincenzo would say.

Typical of the young girls of the post-war period, she had bobbed her hair, much to Rosa's dismay. She wore silk stockings and had shortened all her skirts. She was quick-witted and had become an excellent typist and stenographer. No one in the insurance office where she worked could match her speed and accuracy. In spite of her outward hedonism, she was fiercely family oriented and was devoted to Rosa, who loved being with her energetic daughter; her bright merry ways buoyed Rosa's spirits no end.

After a quiet dinner in the hotel dining room, Philomena suggested going to the Nickelodeon in town. Rosa had never been to a film in her life and was delighted. The feature starred America's Sweetheart, Mary Pickford. Rosa came away so enchanted she vowed to go to the films each week when they returned home.

The next day after breakfast, the two women hastened to the company office on Gilroy Street. Upon entering, they were instructed to wait in the outer office by a svelte-looking secretary who appraised them from head to toe. Undaunted, Philomena sat tapping a slender foot and humming a current tune, much to the disgust of the prim secretary.

After a few minutes a blustery, pompous appearing man burst into the room, puffing on a huge, black cigar. He had wild-looking red hair that stood up on the back of his head in a comical way. In a loud voice he addressed the waiting women.

"Well, well, now ain't this something? Joe and George's folks come to see old John O'Hara," and offering a huge, sweaty palm to Rosa, proceeded to openly admire Philomena's dark beauty.

"I was not aware you knew my sons," answered Rosa, pulling her hand away from this distasteful man.

"Oh, sure, we was old drinking buddies," he laughed hoarsely. "Now, what can I do for you lovely ladies?"

John O'Hara, in spite of his coarse ways, was a shrewd salesman and someone the board at Standard Oil knew could carry out a good deal. He would intimidate the timid, yet could also communicate with the common man. He knew well the value of the large parcel of land Joseph had deeded over to Rosa and Paolo. It was located in the center of one of the richest oil fields in the state and one Standard Oil had long wished to acquire. O'Hara felt he had easy pickings with the two vulnerable women.

"We are interested in selling the plot of land described in this deed," Rosa explained, producing the document made out to Paolo and Rosa.

"We aren't buying much property these days, Missus," O'Hara said with a wily grin that exposed large, yellowed teeth.

"Since you aren't interested, we'll come back in a year or so," snapped Philomena, jumping up from her chair, eager to escape this crude man with the exploring eyes.

"Now, now, little lady, I didn't say we wasn't interested. Just wanted you to know we can't offer much for your property at this time. The market is way down."

"The market is up; this is 1921 and oil prices are booming," retorted Philomena, eyes snapping. Producing a legal-looking document from her purse, she continued, pitching her voice higher to bring home her point.

"I work for John Hancock Insurance and my employer gave me the complete data on oil prices, cost of shares, and financial status of Standard Oil. Now when do we do business?"

Taken aback by this outburst, O'Hara gazed at the young girl with new admiration.

"I will have to read up on today's prices, Miss," O'Hara said.

"You know exactly what today's prices are Mr. O'Hara," came back Philomena sharply.

Damn girl, he thought. She ain't going to be so easy. After scribbling some figures on a pad of paper, he chewed on his cigar and smiled his best smile.

"We could offer something in the neighborhood of $10,000," O'Hara answered slowly, knowing well this figure was ridiculously low.

Philomena threw back her head and gave out a derisive low

laugh, much to the embarrassment of Rosa. O'Hara realized things were getting out of hand and he slowly felt his advantage slipping.

"Fifteen thousand is my top price, little lady," he retorted in a firm tone of voice.

Jumping up from her chair, Philomena slammed her hand on the desk and in a commanding voice responded, "My price is $50,000, take it or leave it!"

Choking on his cigar, O'Hara could feel the blood rushing to his face. He knew full well the land was worth every penny of $50,000, but in no way would that price be offered. This smart-ass minx was a handful and he realized too late he had handled this encounter badly. Trying to regain his composure, he answered in a quieter voice, "I have to consult with my supervisors, ladies. Could I contact you later?"

"We are staying at the Hotel Findlay," Philomena answered sweetly, knowing well her offer had come as a complete surprise.

"Come, Mama, we will go to dinner and wait to hear from Mr. O'Hara." Taking the surprised Rosa by the arm, Philomena sailed out of the office with head high, black curls bobbing. When they were out of sight of the office, Philomena let out a whoop and danced around her mother.

"Didn't we give that old blow-hard his comeuppence, Mama?" Rosa attempted to quiet her enthusiastic daughter, vainly trying to hide a smile, remembering the shocked look on John O'Hara's face. Suddenly she burst into laughter and the two women stood, arms about one another, laughing with sheer abandon.

"Come, Philomena, we must behave ourselves," Rosa said finally, trying to compose herself.

"Oh, Mama, that will live in my memory forever," Philomena said breathlessly, wiping her eyes.

Later that evening after an early dinner, a call came from Standard Oil Company head office. Mr. James Saunders would see them at 8 P.M. regarding the matter at hand. They were to meet Mr. Saunders in the hotel lobby.

Rosa and Philomena, dressed in their finest, waited patiently in the hotel foyer. At precisely 8 p.m. a young man of perhaps thirty, neatly dressed, approached them.

"My name is James Saunders. Do I have the pleasure of addressing Mrs. Cook and her daughter?"

Philomena looked into a pair of gray-green eyes and felt her mouth go dry. Gone was the demeanor of the afternoon and she answered sweetly, "How do you do, Mr. Saunders. Won't you sit down?"

Jim Saunders looked at the two women in surprise. O'Hara's report had been one depicting two very shrewd, conniving women. He saw only two tastefully dressed ladies. The older woman was diminutive, white hair piled high on her head, dressed in a soft, blue silk dress. She had dark eyes and a sweet smile. The younger one was a knock-out, dressed in a pale green frock that revealed shapely long legs. Her black hair was bobbed in the latest fashion and he detected a glimmer of color on her lips. She had a pixie-like face that glowed with animation.

Trying to get his bearings, Jim asked, "Could I interest you ladies in a cup of coffee or refreshment?"

"No, thank you, Mr. Saunders," Rosa answered. "We just finished our dinner." Then she added, "We are anxious to get this matter settled, as we would like to return home in a few days."

Philomena sat silent, a faint smile forming at the corners of her mouth. She had the feeling they had taken this good-looking young man by surprise. She let her mother go on talking, further confusing Jim Saunders. Finally, she spoke in a honey-toned voice, "Would you like to have breakfast with us tomorrow, Mr. Saunders? Perhaps you could show us the sights of the city later in the day."

Not a word about the offer from this one. He found himself answering in the affirmative and before he knew what was happening, they were gone. Damn. O'Hara will be waiting for an answer. If only he had not painted such a distorted picture, I could have drawn my own conclusions. Now, they still have the advantage.

Jim Saunders was an up and coming lawyer. He had worked his way through law school, taking twelve years to complete his studies and finally passing the bar. He supported his widowed mother, with whom he made his home. He had been fortunate to have been entrusted with a great deal of the legal work for Standard Oil. In more delicate matters, such as the Cook case, he was called in to assist in whatever capacity the company felt appropriate.

He now felt a surge of anticipation, he did want to see Miss Cook again. God! She was exciting looking and he whistled a little tune as he made his way back to the office.

O'Hara was there waiting, chewing on the malodorous black cigar.

"Well, what happened?" he roared.

Jim was in too good a mood to have it spoiled by this over-bearing brute. "These things take time, O'Hara, I have to smooth over your blunders," Jim answered slowly, knowing well this answer would only antagonize O'Hara further.

"Listen, you smart-aleck shyster! Don't you forget who makes most of the sales around here," blustered the Irishman.

"Okay, okay, O' Hara, don't break a blood vessel. I'm see-ing them tomorrow and I'm sure we can come to an amicable amount." With that he went out the door.

The following day James met Rosa and Philomena at the ho-tel. After a leisurely breakfast, he drove them through the coun-tryside, pointing out quaint and picturesque old farm houses. It was a cool, crisp day and the air had a hint of coming winter. Leaves of red and gold adorned maple, birch and oak trees. Jim stopped the car beside a lazy brook explaining he had played here as a little boy.

"There's a log cabin up ahead where my parents, my broth-er and I spent two glorious weeks every summer," he explained, pointing in the direction of the cabin.

"Can we see it?" Philomena asked eagerly.

Jim was pleased but dubious. "You may tear your stockings and ruin your shoes. We could come back when you are properly dressed."

He had never shared this spot with anyone except family and now it seemed important he show it to Philomena. He was quite taken with this attractive young woman. She viewed everything with such enthusiasm and had a gay manner. He loved the way her eyes shone when she spoke, lighting up her entire countenance. She conversed intelligently concerning current events of the day and was keenly aware of the political arena.

Rosa had remained silent, drinking in the beauty of the landscape. Whenever she found herself in natural surroundings such as this, her thoughts always reverted back to Paolo. Their walks in Crandall Park came to mind, where they picnicked and sat under the trees while she read to him. How she missed him!

Getting out of the car, she sat on a nearby rock, gazing up into the clear, blue sky. A wave of nostalgia swept over her, and for the first time in her life in America, she longed to see Italy again. She closed her eyes and was mentally transported to her village. Time had clouded the ugliness of her childhood home. She only remembered green valleys, towering mountains and a rushing river. She had no knowledge of the welfare of her family. News of her mother's death had reached her many years ago and her Zio Matteo was probably long dead, too, though no one knew how, where or when.

Rosa wept thinking of the frustration of her mother's life. There had been so little happiness in Maria's world. What could I go home to, thought Rosa. There is nothing there for me, she reasoned. America is my home, where Paolo and I shared a beautiful life together and raised a wonderful family.

She glanced toward Philomena and Jim who were engaged in serious conversation. She smiled watching her young daughter.

Her youngest certainly was filled with the joy of life and seemed to savor every waking moment. She will get what she wants in this life, Rosa mused. And she will achieve the goal she had set out for, the $50,000. Rosa only wanted the money for the purpose of sharing it with her children while they were still young and she could enjoy the giving of such a gift.

On the ride back to the hotel, Philomena and Jim were quiet. Rosa hoped they had not quarreled. She need not have worried for when they reached the hotel, Jim slowly went over to the passenger side of the car. He took Philomena's hand tenderly and helped her alight from the car. They stood silently, facing one another, oblivious of all around them. "Can I see you tonight, Philomena?"

"Yes, Jim."

Rosa let herself out of the car and walked into the hotel. She smiled. My daughter has fallen in love and Rosa's heart sighed again with the beauty of young love.

The next day papers were signed and Rosa was presented with a check for $50,000. She was content and now she was eager to return home. There would be $8,000 for each of her four children. The remaining money would keep her independent for the rest of her life.

On the train ride home it was Rosa who did all the talking. Philomena sat facing the window, watching the rolling countryside, a mysterious smile playing about her mouth. Rosa would have been shocked if she could have read Philomena's mind. She knew she had found the man with whom she wanted to spend the rest of her life. She only had to wait patiently for him to acknowledge what she already felt in her heart.

Jim's eyes had been filled with such longing when they boarded the train. She mentally hugged herself in anticipation of his embrace. She had never played the role of a coquette. She chafed at society's rules of decorum. Were she to follow her instincts she would have readily gone to bed with her new found love. But good sense overcame her desires and she would play the waiting game, albeit restlessly.

Jim in the meantime was uncertain how to break the news to his mother and tell her he was hopelessly in love. After he had put Rosa and Philomena on the train back to Youngstown, he drove around for hours. His mind was in a whirl, his only thoughts were those of dark, flashing eyes lighting up an animated face framed in ebony clouds of curls.

After the excitement created by such a woman, Jim knew he could not endure his mother's quiet ways that evening. His body seemed charged with electric vibrations and he could not calm down. He phoned Mrs. Saunders explaining he would not be home for dinner due to an overload of paper work. He hated lying to his mother, but he had to get a grip on himself. The experience was new to him. One moment he was filled with exhilaration, the next despair.

I want her more than I've ever wanted anything in my life, he thought wildly. Suppose she doesn't want me? She had seemed unhappy to leave this evening, or was that his imagination? He drove dark streets until midnight, trying to sort out his thoughts. Suddenly, he could endure the anxiety no longer and racing back to his office, dialed the Cook residence.

A very sleepy yet alarmed voice answered, "Who is this? Who did you say is calling?" asked Rosa.

"It's James Saunders, Mrs. Cook. I'm sorry to awaken you. Is Philomena home?" he asked nervously.

"Yes, but she's asleep, I think. Is anything wrong?"

"No, nothing's wrong. May I speak to her?" Only my whole life is in the balance, he muttered under his breath.

"Hold on, Mr. Saunders. I will call her," What in the world, thought Rosa.

Philomena heard the words Mr. Saunders and was immediately wide awake. "Jim, is anything wrong?" she was concerned now.

"Philomena I love you. Will you marry me?" He could not

believe he was doing this.

A sweet low laugh, then a breathless, "Yes, oh yes."

"I'm going to come to Youngstown on the next train. I want to hold you and kiss that wonderful face. Am I crazy?" He was laughing and yet there were tears in his eyes.

"Come quickly, Jim. I love you too. And darling, we're both crazy, but it's wonderful!"

Rosa had gone back to her bedroom, but soon heard Philomena running up the stairs calling out, "Mama, Mama, I'm going to be married!"

"Philomena, what are you saying? You hardly know the man. Are you sure?" Rosa stood amazed before her lovestruck daughter.

"Yes, Mama. I've never been so certain of anything in my life."

Rosa gazed keenly at her young daughter and saw the exhilaration and sheer joy in her eyes setting her lovely face aglow. She sighed inwardly. This had been the magic that Paolo had created in my life. How blessed we are. The magical web was encircling Philomena and would create a silken sheath whose warmth would last a lifetime.

CHAPTER 38

A New Venture

Damien and Vincenzo entered into a partnership and reached an agreement. Damien searched for suitable sites for new homes, located the landowners and then purchased the land. Vincenzo obtained the building permits and built sturdy homes. They shared in the profits and soon had gained a solid reputation as a reliable company. A contract was drawn up and P.C. Homes (Palumbo-Cook) gained state-wide attention. Damien never interfered in the designs of such homes knowing Vincenzo's skill along those lines and the latter never questioned his partner's keen sense of location. Thus grew a thriving and very profitable business.

Vincenzo had chosen a lovely site for his new home. It sat atop a slight rise overlooking Newport Lake on the south side of town. He designed the surrounding landscape creating a masterpiece of exterior beauty that blended with the lush surroundings. Gloria outdid herself with all the interior furnishings. She coordinated fabric and color, tiles and textures in intricate mixtures. Vincenzo was more than pleased with the finished results and highly praised his wife.

Gloria's days had been happily filled while planning the furnishing of her new home. When completed she felt a tremendous let down and became bored. She had never learned to cook properly, her attempts were a dismal failure. Vincenzo did not have the time nor inclination to teach her the basic fundamentals of cooking. Gloria begged her husband to hire a cook and he finally agreed after so many disasters on her part. He liked to entertain clients and with the new cook, Josie, their dinner parties were a smashing success.

Gloria made a gorgeous hostess, her blonde beauty reigned supreme. Vincenzo's clients were mostly men in the building trade and the conversation, therefore, always turned to business and Gloria felt incapable of participating. The wives of these men were colorless and boring to her. She longed for a little excitement, but Vincenzo was too wrapped up in his business to pay much heed to her pleading.

She had taken a trip to Florida, leaving Paul in Rosa's care, much to the displeasure of Vincenzo. She was accompanied by a much younger woman and her boyfriend whom Vincenzo did not approve. But Gloria enjoyed herself immensely, swimming every day in the Atlantic and then dancing every night at the hotel. She was not interested in becoming involved romantically with any of her partners, she just wanted a good time. Vincenzo was still a very attractive man, but he had grown stuffy and had forgotten how to have fun. She could not see the harm in enjoying life to its fullest.

When Gloria returned home she realized how much she had missed Paul who adored her. For days after her return he followed her around the house all day. She enjoyed having him so close to her and tried to show her devotion. She played games with him and read stories, acting out all the parts to his childish delight. Squeals of laughter rang throughout the house and Vincenzo had to smile in spite of himself.

She could still arouse her husband, which she did frequently when Paul was safely asleep. Gloria would appear before Vincenzo, bathed and perfumed, long hair falling about her face. He was constantly amazed at her frenzied passion and their love-making reached such a crescendo that he would be utterly exhausted. It was moments such as this he professed his love. In the light of day, however, their differences became apparent.

Vincenzo knew a solution had to be found if the marriage was to endure.

A theater group was being formed in Youngstown and large ads were displayed in the evening newspaper, The Telegram. Gloria read the ads with a great deal of interest and wondered, did she dare answer the ad? She had no acting experience but she knew she could learn. Eager to try, the next day she dropped Paul off at Rosa's. She dressed in her finest, and brushed her hair until it shone. She made a striking appearance and her regal beauty did not go unnoticed.

Tim Nolan had high hopes for a legitimate theater in Youngstown. He had very little money and could not afford to rent an appropriate theater. His wartime buddy, Jack Nicols, had a farmhouse on the outskirts of town. He also had a large, unused barn which he agreed to rent to Tim for his theater group. The rent was minimal, a paltry fifteen dollars a month, enough to pay the taxes, Jack had said.

Tim spent weeks painting and refurbishing the old barn with Jack's help. They rigged up a stage and made a curtain from materials they found in an old cedar chest in the attic. "Now all we need are actors, Jack," said Tom, admiring their handiwork.

"They'll come, mark my words," Jack answered. And come they did. Shakespearean actors, musical comedy has-beens, comics, and a few old vaudevillians. Not a first-class actor in the lot. But Tim was not discouraged, these things take time, he mused. Maybe I'll get lucky and a gem will drop by. It was on that very day Gloria Cook walked into his life.

Tim discovered Gloria had never acted in her life. With her beauty, he told Jack later, she could read the phone book and keep men awestruck. And so began Gloria's acting career with Tim Nolan her eager teacher. Surprisingly, Gloria blossomed under his tutelage and within a few short months he was ready to introduce his new-found protegé in a small part in an Ibsen play, *Love's Comedy*.

Gloria's long trips out to the barn four days a week were creating a serious problem. Each day she dropped Paul off at Rosa's, much to her small son's disappointment. He loved Rosa but missed his mother's attention and previous show of devotion. He became morose as the weeks went by. Soon Vincenzo noticed Paul's quiet ways and questioned Gloria.

"He's just going through a phase, dear," she answered in an off-hand manner.

Gloria had not revealed the acting lessons to anyone. She had never been so happy and looked forward to each new day. Now that she had a part in a play, she must inform Vincenzo and she was loathe to do so. Tonight was dress rehearsal and she had left Paul at Rosa's to stay overnight. After dinner she approached Vincenzo. She knew his immediate reaction would be one of shock and surprise. But she did not anticipate the angry and heated discussion that followed.

"What do you mean you are in a play? What play? Whatever are you talking about?" An angry and impatient tone had begun to creep into his voice.

"It's a theater group recently formed and I have been taking acting lessons."

"Acting lessons! Gloria, I don't know what you are talking about. How could you be taking acting lessons?"

"I've been going to the theater four days a week"

"Four days a week! Who has been taking care of Paul?" Vincenzo was now losing control and felt the blood rushing to his face.

"Your mother takes good care of Paul." Gloria was now in a defensive mood.

"Paul is our son and I expect you to take care of him, not my mother! How could you go gallivanting around town and neglect your child?"

"He's not neglected. You always said yourself what a wonderful mother Rosa is." Gloria was beginning to tremble. She had never seen Vincenzo so angry.

"You are not going to be in any play. Do you hear me?" The very thought of his wife parading around in some broken-down theater filled him with disgust. How could she shame me this way?

"You sound just like my father," Gloria spoke up harshly.

"You're a woman, Gloria, not a young star-struck girl. You will do as I ask." Vincenzo was adamant and stood staring at his wife, fists clenched at his sides. Gloria turned sharply and ran upstairs to their bedroom. Vincenzo heard the door slam shut and the key being turned in the lock.

Furiously he left, distraught and confused. He headed for Rosa's house to pick up Paul. Rosa heard her son come through the front door and rose to greet him. His face was ashen and she drew her breath in sharply. "Vincenzo, what is wrong?"

He went over to the divan and sat with his head in his hands. Slowly, he described the argument that had taken place. "What am I to do, Mama? How can she cheapen herself so?" he asked in an anguished voice. "Why can't she be happy with her home and Paul? I've given her a lovely home and her own car."

"Apparently she needs more, son. You have your business, which you love. Perhaps acting gives her some stimulation, have you thought about that?"

Vicenzo looked at his mother in a perplexed way. "But Mama, you never needed outside stimulation, as you put it."

"I had a big family. Also, I had so much to learn, having come from another country. I had my studies which I loved. What excites Gloria besides you and Paul?" she asked kindly.

"You think I'm wrong then. Asking my wife not to perform in a cheap play?"

"I think you ordered her," reminded Rosa. "But I do agree she acted impulsively and unwisely. Would you like me to talk with her and act as mediator?"

Vincenzo threw up his hands in despair. "Things couldn't

be much worse." He gathered up his sleeping son from Rosa's big bed, being careful not to awaken the boy. He then drove his mother and son to his home. He put Paul to bed and returned to the kitchen where Rosa was making coffee.

"I'll go up and talk with Gloria," Rosa said. Tapping gently on the bedroom door, Rosa spoke in a low voice to her daughter-in-law. Vincenzo heard the key turn in the lock and the bedroom door being opened and then shut again.

Two hours later, a smiling, but weary Rosa came downstairs and into the kitchen. "I drank a whole pot of coffee, Mama. I'll probably be awake for a week," he laughed nervously.

Rosa took her son's face in her hands. Kissing him gently, she smiled and said in a low voice, "Your wife will give up her acting. But you must see to her needs. I think we have found a solution."

"You know I love her, Mama. Anything within reason."

"She wants to be more than a housewife and mother. This is my plan, Vincenzo. And before you say no, I want you to care-fully consider what I am about to say." Rosa laid out her plan, speaking slowly and with conviction. Vincenzo at first began to balk, but Rosa continued, paying him no heed. The plan was truly one of great possibilities.

Gloria had wonderful style and sense of color. Vincenzo built great houses, but when completed, they were bare and unimag-inative. Gloria could decorate several, giving prospective buyers a visual aid, and be present when the houses were being shown, offering professional advice when needed.

Vincenzo looked at his mother in amazement. How could she have dreamed up such a marvelous idea? Gloria did not appear in the play, her understudy went on in her place. The play was a hit, much to Gloria's relief. She never saw Tim Nolan again.

Gloria began her role as an interior decorator. The arrange-ment became such a success that she was in great demand. Vincenzo's pride in his wife's new endeavor grew to where she became a third partner in the business.

Petals from a Rose

CHAPTER 39

A Fine Wedding

Philomena had fulfilled all her mother's desires for a beautiful wedding and Rosa was in her element. St. Joseph's Church was filled with baskets of flowers and the altar was a bower of pink and white roses. Philomena's wedding gown was lavish in satin and lace with a train seven feet long. The bodice was embellished with tiny satin rosettes and in the center of each was a tiny pearl. Her veil swept beyond the long train of her gown, and the headdress consisted of a large crown of satin rosettes that framed her black curls. There were six bridesmaids, one of whom was Christina.

"This is like a beauty pageant," laughed Vincenzo as he greeted them at the back of the church.

The bridesmaids wore long silk pink gowns and floppy pink straw hats, each girl carried a small bouquet of pink and white roses. Maria, still a beautiful woman in her early forties, was her sister's matron of honor and was dressed in a pale mauve gown. Rosa, handsome in blue chiffon, wore a small band of pink flowers identical to Maria's. Each band was intricately attached to a veil that fitted tightly to their heads.

The entire family had spent the previous day decorating the church's new reception hall. White cloths covered the tables and a vase of pink roses graced each one. The ladies of the parish had spent days preparing the feast that was to follow the Nuptial Mass. A small orchestra had been hired and sat ready for the arrival of the happy couple.

Olga Saunders had immediately fallen in love with Philomena, sensing this high-spirited girl would be an asset to her son's career. Already, the girl had mentioned Jim running for political office. She was just what James needed in his too quiet life. She was not that enthused over the ostentatious wedding Mrs. Cook had arranged, but it did bring to the wedding her older son, Evan, and his snooty wife, Roslyn. She had not seen Evan for almost a year, his wife kept him too busy with all her social affairs. Evan was an orthopedic surgeon and had a large practice. Olga was deeply disappointed the marriage had not produced the grandchildren she so wanted. She hoped Philomena would fill that void.

Jason Stone had slipped into the back of the church unnoticed. As he sat watching the bridesmaids file down the aisle to the strains of the wedding march, his heart leaped at the sight of Christina. He had only eyes for her.

Evan had observed the young man, who desperately tried to keep himself hidden. He was especially mindful of the brace the lad wore on his left leg.   After the ceremony, he tried unsuccessfully to seek out the sad-looking fellow. Later at the reception, he cornered his brother James.

"Congratulations, little brother! Looks like you captured quite a filly," Evan said as he pumped Jim' s hand.

"She's the best thing that ever happened to me, Evan," answered Jim beaming.

"Where the hell did she get a name like Philomena? Sounds like an opera." Evan laughed, sipping on a glass of champagne.

"I know. I just call her Phil," smiled Jim.

"How does she feel about moving in with Mom?" he whispered.

"That's one of the things I love about the girl," Jim answered. "Just as though there was never any question about the whole situation, she's accepted Mom beautifully. I think the two of them will get along just fine."

"Hooray for you, old man, you deserve only the best. Say, tell me, Jim, who is the young fellow with the brace? I looked for him after the ceremony, but I guess he ran for cover."

"Oh, that's Jason Stone. He's an art teacher who works for my new sister-in-law, Maria."

"What was his problem?"

"He had infantile paralysis at the age of nine. Left him with a bad leg. Why the interest?"

"You know me, Jim. Can't bear to see anyone going through life crippled if I can help it," Evan answered.

It was true. Evan sought out charity cases as he charged the wealthy larger sums so he could feel free to aid someone less fortunate. This he kept from his wife. Roslyn didn't have a charitable bone in her body. He made a point to seek out Philomena's family, wanting to discover more about Jason.

Vincenzo gave Philomena away, and as he walked down the aisle with his lovely sister, he noted Gloria and Paul sitting in the back of the church. He was quite disturbed by this as the family members were to sit in the front pew. Calling Gloria aside after the ceremony, he asked, "Gloria, why were you sitting in the back of the church?"

"Paul was not feeling well and I wanted to be able to leave in case he became worse," she answered in a worried voice.

"What's wrong with him? He seemed all right earlier in the day."

"He must have something on his mind. He keeps looking over his shoulder all the time, fidgets and breaks out in tears when I ask what's wrong."

"I had better have a talk with him," Vincenzo promised.

Paul was not a happy child and when he started school that year his behavior became erratic. He hated the restrictions of the classroom as he was accustomed to having the run of his parent's home in their absence. They both worked and Josie, the cook, tried to discipline him but to no avail; he was the master of the house when his mother and father were not at home. He was docile in their presence, therefore, they had no inkling of any problems. Josie would not complain to them fearful of losing her job for which she was paid handsomely.

Now with Paul in school most of the day, Josie's life was much easier. She managed to take an hour nap each day before he returned home and was thus fortified for his mischievous ways. Lately, however, when he came in from school he began to stay in his room with the door locked. At first Josie was thrilled he was not giving her any trouble, but as the ritual continued she began to be uneasy. The quiet unnerved her and one day she knocked on his door when she smelled smoke.

"Paul, what are you doing in there?" Josie nervously asked.

"Go away, leave me alone!"

"Are you playing with matches? If you are, I'm going to tell your father," she threatened.

Slowly the door opened a crack and Paul answered with a snarl, "You better not tell my father! You'll be sorry if you ever say anything!"

Josie was frightened by his voice and said, "I won't say anything, but don't let me catch you playing with matches." She turned and went downstairs promising herself she would talk with her brother, Henry, as to what method she should use to control Paul.

Henry was not sympathetic towards Paul and told Josie the boy needed a good thrashing by his father. He agreed to come over to the house when Paul returned from school and talk with him, and if that did not work, he argued the boy needed good old-fashioned discipline by his father.

A few days later when Paul returned home from school, Henry was sitting in the kitchen having a cup of coffee with Josie. Henry was a rough looking man who had worked with his hands as a mechanic and his nails were always filled with grease, a sight that filled Paul with nausea. Henry stood up and addressed the young boy. "Josie tells me you play with matches."

"I do not!"

"You know what happens to little boys who lie, don't you?"

"You had better leave my father's house if you know what's good for you," threatened Paul, with his hands clenched into fists.

Waves of anger flowed over Henry. He was a man who had been forced to quit school in the fourth grade to go to work in a shoe factory to help feed his brothers and sisters. Here was a boy that had everything and was spoiled rotten, even giving Josie a hard time.

Grabbing Paul by the arm he sneered, "What you gonna do, big man, if I don't?"

"Josie, make him let go of me!" Paul whimpered.

"Henry, let him go," Josie was fast becoming alarmed by this turn of events.

"I'll be watching you, laddie, and if you give Josie a bad time, I'll come after you."

Paul slipped from Henry's grasp and ran to his room and locked the door. "Now, you've done it, Henry," wailed Josie. "Supposing he tells his dad?"

"That kid ain't gonna say anything to anyone, mark my words. He's nothing but a spoiled brat!" Henry hitched up his pants and left, muttering to himself about the injustice of life.

For days Josie lived in fear Paul would tell Mr. Cook and she would be fired. Josie loved this job working in such a fine home. It was clean work, she always told her brothers and sisters. A cleaning woman came in every Monday and did all the hard scrubbing, laundry and ironing. Mrs. Cook treated her well and was not too demanding.

Josie was overly indulgent with Paul in the days that followed Henry's threat. She packed him delicious lunches filled with extra fruit and candy. But Paul gave most of his lunches to grateful fellow students and continued to shut himself away in his room on his return home from school.

It was true, Paul had been playing with matches, he loved the blue flame they created and watched fascinated when he lighted some papers in his wastebasket. If only he had more space to indulge his new-found pleasure!

After the wedding when everyone was leaving, Damien approached Vincenzo. "Hey, Vinnie, I've been wanting talk with you all day long. I have a client who wants to build a shopping mall here in Youngstown. It's quite a new idea and I'm pretty excited about it. He wants us to meet him early tomorrow. Can you get away?"

"Sure, Damien, sounds great," Vincenzo answered, all thoughts of talking with Paul gone.

Paul watched his parents activities carefully the next few days. They left together each morning, Vincenzo driving Gloria to the office. They always left the garage door closed but unlocked. There was nothing in the garage of any value, just some gardening tools, old glass jars and some empty flower pots. These pots were cement and quite heavy and ornate; Vincenzo meant to get rid of them.

Wednesday, the day before Thanksgiving, Josie was busy in the kitchen baking pies and preparing the stuffing for the 26 lb turkey she would bake the following day. There were hors d'ouevres to make and special sauces, so she was not mindful of Paul quietly slipping out of the house and into the garage.

At last! Here I can really have all the room I need, thought Paul gleefully. All week long he had saved the daily newspaper. These he kept hidden in the garage. Paul emptied the bag holding the papers and began crumpling up each sheet into a large, round piece until he had many balls of paper. Now he was ready.

Striking a match he watched the pile of newspapers catch fire. He stood transfixed before the blue and red flames, his eyes glowing with the picture before him. The fire grew larger and larger. One flame flew out and landed on his shirt; it caught Paul off guard. He ran to the door, tripped, fell against one of the heavy cement vases and was knocked unconscious.

A neighbor passing by saw the smoke and ran to the garage

door, but it was too hot for him to open up.

"Fire! Fire!" he shouted.

Josie heard him and called the fire department, then ran to the garage unaware Paul was inside. She could not open the door either. The fire truck arrived within minutes and the firemen tore open the garage door. There was Paul lying just a few feet away from the flames. She screamed in horror. A fireman rushed to the unconscious boy, pulling him away from the flames. Fortunately, they had arrived in the nick of time. Paul was mostly unharmed, only one side of his face was scorched. It could have been much worse.

Hearing of the fire, Vincenzeo rushed home and saw Paul lying on a guerney. He clutched the frightened boy to his chest, tears running down his face unabated. The fury within Vincenzo was almost unbearable to watch. "I could have lost my son!"

Vincenzo informed Gloria their marriage was at an end. He would provide for her, but never wanted to see her again. Gloria, unhappy in her marriage, always restless and never satisfied, agreed and departed to Florida to live with a girlfriend, promising Paul he could come and visit. Vincenzo sold their beautiful home and neither father nor son, despite her promises, ever saw Gloria again.

Damien located a ranch in the hills, put down a sizable amount of money, and rented the house to Vincenzo, a quiet haven for Paul to recuperate from his near disaster. He and Vincenzo closed up their shop temporarily, giving Vincenzo time to spend with his son after realizing the boy needed his father.

He bought Paul a gold and white Collie, bringing it into his room. Paul was overjoyed as he nuzzled the lovely canine; he called him Prince. The dog never left his side. A bond was gradually formed between father and son. Damien arranged camping trips for them all and the sight of Paul and his father putting up their tent brought tears to his eyes.

CHAPTER 40

Jason

Damien was an integral part of Maria's life, his very presence enriched her as well as her children. He had convinced Maria that Frankie should play high school football. Discovering Christina had a fine singing voice, he hired a music coach. The children had never been so happy and they adored Damien. Later that year, it was no surprise to anyone when Damien and Maria were quietly married in St. Joseph's Church. Frankie gave his mother away and Christina acted as her mother's maid-of-honor.

The new family moved into a fine home on the South Side located two blocks from Mill Creek Park. Every Saturday, Damien and Frankie went fishing on one of the three lakes. On Sundays during the summer months Maria packed a picnic lunch and the four of them hiked through the park. Never had Damien been so happy. He worshiped Maria and she returned his love with sheer abandon. At long last Damien had the family he had wanted all his life.

Christina had shown great promise. She possessed a powerful operatic voice and with the proper training could go on to a successful career. No one was as enthusiastic as Damien. He saw to her diet, insisting on the proper foods. No fats or sugars were allowed. Fresh fruits and vegetables had to be served every day. He gave her breathing lessons himself, a task reminiscent of his coaching days. Christina obeyed him completely and strove for perfection. She loved singing and aspired to acceptance in the Metropolitan Opera.

Damien had purchased season tickets to the Metropolitan in Cleveland for the entire family. What a thrill it was to dress in their finest and be a part of such grandeur. They listened in rapt attention to virtuosos like Lawrence Tibbett and John McCormack and thrilled to the rich tones of Grace Moore and Lily Pons. Lily Pons was Christina's favorite, as she was dark and tiny like herself and possessed one of the finest soprano voices in the country.

In his senior year Frankie became a star football player. Maria winced each time he returned home from practice with bruises, cuts and scrapes all over his body. The entire family attended all the high school football games loudly cheering for Frankie. Damien could not have been prouder if Frankie had been his own son. Upon graduation, Frankie enrolled in Oberlin College with architecture as his major. He aspired to follow in Vincenzo's footsteps, his uncle promising him a place in the business when he obtained his bachelor's degree.

Damien suggested Maria leave John Hancock and help him set up a studio to display his father's paintings. This gave her great satisfaction and she loved working in the studio. Meeting new artists and displaying their works made her eager to devote most of her time to the studio. She talked with Damien regarding holding art classes once a week in the back room of the studio. She felt she might hire an art teacher who could instruct young children. Damien agreed and a sign was placed in the window calling for an art teacher.

Several young people applied, one of whom touched Maria's heart. He was a young man in his twenties with the most expressive green eyes she had ever seen. He told her his name was Jason Stone. Maria hesitated momentarily. This young man was handicapped. He wore a heavy metal brace on one leg and his walking was laborious. He carried a briefcase from which he drew out a bundle of paintings. They were watercolors and Maria looked at them in amazement.

"These are beautiful. When did you do them?" Maria asked.

"Several years ago, " he answered softly.

"Did you take lessons Jason?"

"No, Ma'am. I just started painting one day."

"I can see you enjoy painting. You are very creative."

"Thank you. I really need this job. I think I could be a good teacher." He spoke slowly and Maria knew he was being truthful about needing the job.

"When can you start, Jason?"

He answered eagerly, "As soon as you want me."

"May I display some of your watercolors here in the studio, Jason?" Maria asked, looking through his paintings once again.

"Do you think they are good enough?"

Maria could see he was hesitant about displaying his works and replied, "If you would rather not, I will understand. Oh, and Jason, I'm sorry the pay is so small. Perhaps as time goes on we can raise it a bit," she added apologetically.

"It's alright, Mrs. Palumbo. Thank you for giving me a chance to prove myself. I will see you tomorrow and we can go over your plans." He painstakingly withdrew, a bright smile lighting his somber face.

Maria sat down in the middle of the studio and tears clouded her eyes. What a heartbreak the mother of this young man must endure she thought. She tried to imagine Frankie in similar circumstances, and could not picture such sadness. Why had God chosen Jason to show other young men how fortunate they were? She went about heavy-hearted all day, Jason's face before her. But how he could paint! Perhaps this was God's reward for the cross he had to bear. Maria hoped so.

Jason threw himself into his new job, bringing color and excitement to the quiet studio. Young children watched fascinated as he created with a swoop of his paintbrush, blue skies, green trees, brilliant flowers and animals of every stripe and hue. Soon they were imitating his unique style and Maria was astounded by such a show of talent.

Shyly, Jason consented to Maria's desire to display two of his best watercolors in the main studio. He was overjoyed when a small piece appeared in the evening paper under the heading, Art World, praising his style. He had clipped it out of the paper and carried it proudly in his shirt pocket.

He never spoke of family, but Maria did learn he lived alone in an old house not far from town. He subsisted on a small inheritance left to him by his grandmother. Maria was happy she could contribute in a small way to his limited finances.

Months went by. The art class had grown to ten children, ranging in ages from twelve to sixteen. Jason had complete command of the young people and they worked in earnest, always asking advice on the mixing of colors and correct procedure. He earned their respect by praising all their efforts and offering advice on how to better their techniques.

It was his idea to hold a showing in time for the Christmas holidays. The children were delighted and Christina and Frankie offered to decorate the studio. Maria provided red bows, pine cones, and evergreen boughs, and Rosa promised to bake cookies and prepare sugared nuts for the occasion. The event was to be held on the first Sunday in December. Each child's best work was displayed throughout the studio.

The happy day arrived and no one was as nervous as Jason. The art students had brought their parents and family friends, and soon the small studio was filled to overflowing. A light snow was falling lending a holiday spirit to the event.

People entered, red-cheeked, shaking snow from their clothing. Jason came alone. He always traveled by street car, which fortunately stopped two doors away from the studio. The conductor had grown to admire the courageous young man, and when the weather was inclement such as today, he would stop in front of the studio.

Christina and Frankie went among the guests offering cookies and nuts. Parents were in a happy mood, exclaiming over each child's display. An elderly man took Maria aside and offered to purchase Jason's watercolors for a handsome price.

Maria crossed the room to where Jason was talking with the father of one of his students. She overheard the parent explaining to Jason that his son's grades at school had improved. The father attributed it to the awakening his son had experienced from his art classes for it somehow had spilled over into the academic portion of his schooling. Jason agreed, pointing out that Billy's painting was exceptional. He was able to create beauty all on his own, drawing out a talent that had gone unobserved before. Jason always praised Billy highly, encouraging him to express himself without any inhibitions.

Maria waited until Jason and Billy's father finished their conversation. She now spoke. "Jason, may I talk with you privately for a minute?"

"Of course, Mrs. Palumbo. Everything is going so well," he beamed, his eyes glowing with pride.

"Yes, and I am so pleased. I have a buyer for your watercolors. Do you want to sell them? He is offering a substantial amount."

He hesitated momentarily. "My paintings are like my children, it's so hard to give them up. But I do need the money," he sighed.

"Would you like to meet the gentleman, Jason?"

"No, please. Will you handle the transaction and thank him for me?" He hurried off into the back room.

Christina found him there later when she needed to replenish her supply of nuts and cookies. He was sitting alone in the dark.

"Oh, you startled me, Jason. I didn't know anyone was here."

Christina had grown fond of this young man. His eyes were so painfully beautiful and sad. Now that the party seemed to draw him out somewhat, she hoped to invite him to her parent's home for Christmas dinner. She knew he had no living relatives and the Cook family was so large, another place at table would not upset any plans.

Her voice stirred all the longing in his tortured soul and his heart wept for a love that never could be his. He hated his crippled leg, feeling no woman would ever want him. He shut out dreams that forever were in his mind and plugged into his work with a frenzy.

Jason's parents had been killed in a terrible car accident leaving the young boy in the care of his grandmother, Martha Stone, who had been a widow for 18 years. The shock was almost more than he could bear and his grandma tried to make a home for him.

On awakening one morning not long after his ninth birthday, Jason had been unable to move his legs, and falling to the floor, cried out, "Grandma! What is happening to me?"

An outbreak of the viral disease poliomyelitis swept throughout the country. It affected mostly children, but it struck adults too. The malady for Jason was one he endured for three years. He was in a wheelchair, but determined to walk. When he saw many children hospitalized in iron lungs, he wept for them.

One day Grandma Stone came into his room holding a newspaper in her hand. "Jason, honey, I want to show you something that may interest you and give you hope." She opened up the newspaper showing a picture of a man in a wheelchair. Beneath the picture was a story about this man, a political leader and statesman; his name was Franklin Delano Roosevelt and he had a huge smile. He waved at reporters and all those who had come to see him even though they too were in wheelchairs. FDR had overcome the worst of the disease due to his amazing will-power and would later become the 32nd President of the United States.

Jason read the article over and over, thinking what if he could be as courageous as Franklin Delano Roosevelt? He had great hope.

Martha Stone bought paint, brushes and art paper, always encouraging Jason to pour out his grief on canvas. His first attempts were grotesque, these were the symbols of his black moods, the mind pictures conjured up by his anguish.

Little by little, with Grandma Stone's love and patience, he worked through his pain and after two years was able to walk unaided except for the heavy metal brace but although ambulatory, he always felt awkward. His afflicted leg having grown less than the other, he limped visibly.

Slowly, the pictures he painted began to soften in concept. Gone were the blacks and somber greys, in their place yellow and green, scarlet and gold colors appeared. One large room had been arranged as his studio and Martha Stone hired a carpenter who installed a skylight. Here Jason could catch all the light of the day; he spent hours lost in creativity.

Martha Stone had become weary after years of caring for Jason, exhausting days aggravated all the more with her growing age. She remained cheerful for her grandson's sake, but finally her body succumbed to all the efforts and one morning she was found in her peaceful sleep. She left Jason a sizable legacy she had saved from her husband and Jason remained in the home they had shared, which he now owned.

Jason grieved daily for his grandmother. She had been a real mother to him. One day he spied an article in the local newspaper for an artist to work with young children, to teach them the joy of painting. In anticipation he answered the ad and was hired by Marie Palumbo; theirs was a friendship that blossomed almost immediately.

CHAPTER 41

Christina

*J*ason, it seemed, had disappeared. None but Marie Palumbo knew his whereabouts and she was solemnly sworn to secrecy by Jason; she had given her word and though difficult as it was, kept his secret. Unknowing of the true facts, Christina looked for him but after two years, came to the sad conclusion he might never return.

She had no interest in young men her age and devoted all of her energies to her music. She had graduated from high school and now her training became more arduous. She had entered many contests in the past two years and always emerged victorious. Her voice had matured and grown stronger each year.

Her singing had a quality difficult to define, clear and vibrant, but with a hint of sadness. Perhaps it was this quality that gave her so much appeal, opera itself has always been filled with tales of sorrow. Christina's roles took on such a believable quality, she seemed to live the characters she portrayed, as though she was searching through her songs to find an answer to her own heavy heart.

A great opportunity had arisen. A scout for the Metropolitan Opera was to hold auditions at the Stambaugh Auditorium. Christina was asked to participate and she answered with great excitement. She had chosen the opera, *Turandot* by Puccini, and she would play the role of Lui.

Of all the hopeful entrants, only Christina imparted such a moving performance. Her sweetly lyrical voice, coupled with her shy demeanor and diminutive size, made Lui a very sympathetic and tragic figure. Her two arias displayed such gripping sensitivity and intelligence of character, she easily met the standard of excellence.

Maestro Fiorelli had slipped into the auditorium unobserved. From his seat in the back of the auditorium he listened to Christina's magnificent performance; he was deeply moved. Such a voice! This was truly star quality and he hastened to his hotel to call his friend, Oscar Brandon, head of the Metropolitan in Cleveland.

The audition brought to the Metropolitan two new stars, Christina, and the tenor Emilio Mastroianni. It was a dream come true. Maria and Damien could not believe their daughter's good fortune. But no one could have been happier than Rosa. Her heart swelled with pride at her granddaughter's achievement.

It was necessary that Christina take up residence in Cleveland and she begged Rosa live with her for the time, being as she could not bear to be alone. Maria and Damien were unable at that time to leave Youngstown for business reasons so Rosa became the logical choice. She agreed to a three month's stay, hoping a different solution would appear. She dreaded being away from her home.

The big, old house that Paolo had so lovingly built for his family was beginning to show signs of neglect. The neighborhood had become run-down and Vincenzo and Maria begged Rosa to sell the house and come live with either of them. But she would not leave, saying she must stay where she and Paolo had raised their family. Her eyes saw only a beautiful home. Paolo dwelled in every room and she found comfort feeling his presence. Now that she was all alone she began talking to him as though he were present. She had to be careful the children did not hear these conversations, they would think her senile.

Christina needed her so she resolutely packed her bags. She was loathe to go and made Vincenzo promise he would look after the house and care for Paolo's roses. Three months seemed like such a long time. She had scrubbed and cleaned every room and had washed all the windows until they shone. The white ruffled curtains had been starched and ironed and the kitchen floor waxed and polished. This home was her jewel, her pride and joy.

Rosa sighed as she locked the front door and stood on the porch waiting for Damien to pick her up. Seeing the smiles on the faces of Damien, Maria and Christina as they drove up, she put her unhappy thoughts behind her. Rosa did not want to put a damper on the occasion.

"Grandma, we'll have a wonderful time!" Christina happily exclaimed, as she kissed her grandmother.

"Of course we will, dear," Rosa answered putting on a cheerful face. "I will be a lady of leisure."

Maria was relieved her mother had accepted this role so well. She felt the change would be good for her, Rosa had kept to herself too much lately. She was grateful that at seventy-three Rosa was still an active and healthy woman. She knew, too, that Rosa missed Philomena, her sister had kept Rosa busy and cheerful.

Philomena and Jim had made their home in Findlay with Jim's mother, Olga. The union had produced two children in three years with a third on the way. Philomena was determined to have a large family and she was truly the typical, efficient hausfrau. Jim was a proud and happy husband and father.

Jim's law practice was quite successful and now he had entered the race for councilman of his district. Philomena, despite her pregnancy, was his active campaign manager. Olga adored the children and happily took on the chore of caring for them while Philomena was on Jim's campaign trail. Theirs was a happy household. Because of the distance, Rosa was unable to see the grandchildren as often as she liked and she felt cheated of the opportunity to be close to them.

Christina's life became a round of lessons, rehearsals and stage work. Each night, weary and discouraged, she hastened to the apartment where Rosa always had a hot meal waiting. She was to appear in the opera *Madame Butterfly*, a role she had long hoped to portray. But the hours were long and tedious and she sometimes wondered if this was indeed her life's dream. The pursuit of the golden chalice of fame and success was an exhausting one. She discovered she must use musical muscles and dramatic strengths she never knew she possessed. The stage work was grueling and many days she was reduced to tears.

Then, suddenly, triumph was around the corner. Opening night was just before Thanksgiving. It was to be her first starring role. The turmoil within her could no longer be hidden and one week before her performance, she was running a high fever. Quickly, Rosa summoned a doctor who informed her Christina had pneumonia. He put her in a hospital immediately with a nurse in attendance around the clock.

Tearfully, Rosa called Maria, urging her to come quickly. Maria and Damien drove frantically over icy highways to be at her bedside. They were met by Rosa whose tear-stained face showed visible signs of fatigue. Maria was filled with remorse for placing her mother in such a trying situation.

Maria and Damien sat beside Christina's bed all night. Frankie arrived in the early dawn and took Rosa back to the apartment. He insisted she lie down for some much needed sleep. "Promise you will call me if you get any news from the hospital," pleaded Rosa.

"I will, Grandma. I promise," he answered, trying to fight back the tears.

The doctor had given Christina medication that put her in a deep sleep. She dreamed of Jason and he was walking towards her. He was not wearing the heavy metal brace on his leg but was straight and tall, walking firm and steady. She held out her hand to him and he clasped it tightly in his. Then he leaned over her and kissed her gently on the lips. The dream was so real! She could feel the softness of his mouth on hers.

She slept peacefully then and by noon the next day her fever had dropped to 102 degrees. When she awakened Maria was standing over her, tears in her eyes. "Christina, baby, we're here," she whispered, brushing back wet black curls from the pale face.

"Mama, I'm so sorry," she cried.

"Sorry! All we want is for you to be well," Damien blurted out. "When you are well you're coming back home with us."

"But my contract with the Metropolitan?" she groaned.

"That's all taken care of, baby. We'll talk about it when you are better," Maria explained, holding tightly to Christina's hand.

"Is Grandma okay? Poor dear, she was so frightened," cried Christina, her eyes full of tears.

"Yes, dear, she's fine. Frankie took her to the apartment and put her to bed."

"I had the strangest dream, Mama. I dreamed of Jason and he wasn't wearing the brace on his leg."

"It was no dream, Christina," said a low voice from behind Maria.

Jason walked slowly towards the bed, a bright smile on his face. The room seemed to come alive reflecting the rapture on Christina's face. She was speechless with joy and held out her arms to the shy, young man. "Oh, Jason, I'm so happy you are here," she cried out as she wrapped her arms about him. "Where did you go and how is it you are here?"

"It's a long story. You must rest now and when you are stronger, I'll tell you everything."

"You won't go away again? Promise!" she pleaded.

"I promise. I'll never leave you again," he answered softly.

With that she lay back on her pillow and slept peacefully, a sweet smile on her wan face.

At Philomena and Jim's wedding reception, Dr. Evan Saunders had obtained Jason's address from Maria. The next day was Sunday and on a pretext of calling on an old friend, he visited Jason at his home. The plan he presented to Jason was a daring one.

"It's a new procedure we are working on, Jason," he explained solemnly. "The process will take many operations and two years. Are you willing to try?"

"Dr. Saunders," Jason stammered, "I want it more than anything. But I cannot pay, I'm a poor man."

"Let me worry about that, son. When can you leave?"

"Immediately!" was the eager reply.

"Here's my office address and phone number," Dr. Saunders said, handing him a business card. "As soon as you get into town, we'll get you set up at the hospital."

"I will be indebted to you all my life," whispered Jason, fighting back the tears that welled up in his eyes,

"Now, now, laddie, you'll be doing the profession a great service."

Jason could hardly believe his good fortune. He packed a small suitcase and closed up the house. He would be gone two years into a journey of pain and expectation, with the daily hope all would be well. He swore Marie to secrecy begging her not to tell Christina, for fear of failure and disappointment.

Hospitals were practically empty in 1925 and Dr. Saunders had placed Jason on the third floor where he had two rooms all to himself. Dr. Saunders brought paint and canvasses to Jason to help occupy his painful days.

Beautiful works of art appeared in the vestibule of the hospital and soon visitors were eagerly buying up the colorful paintings by the mysterious artist who was the patient, Jason. Several paintings featured the face of a beautiful young girl with long, black curls and startling blue eyes. These Dr. Saunders would not sell.

Jason had drawn from his memory the lovely face of Christina, creating a dreamlike quality to his canvas. As one visitor exclaimed, when he studied a large painting of the unknown girl, "A person could get lost in those magnificent blue eyes!" Try as he would, he could not purchase the lovely painting.

There were many landscapes with their muted pastels, snow

scenes with children merrily playing, and scenes of rushing streams bordered with wild flowers. The same visitor found Dr. Saunders in his office and questioned him. "Somehow, I think I know this artist. I bought two watercolors a couple of years ago from a young man. This artist has the same style. Is his name Jason Stone?"

"I really am not at liberty to say," Dr. Saunders explained carefully.

The visitor smiled. He was sure the artist was the same man whose watercolors hung in his library. He left the hospital with six more paintings and placed them carefully in the trunk of his car. He was to become the owner of the largest collection of paintings by the future famous artist, Jason Stone.

All monies garnered from the sale of the paintings went towards the hospital expenses. Dr. Saunders would not accept any payment. His admiration for the courageous young man grew as the months wore on. Never a word of complaint was heard even though Dr. Saunders knew the man was in pain much of the time. Never was any human being any more deserving of a normal life. It was to this end the good doctor worked steadily, trying every technique he and his colleagues could perform.

When the series of operations had been completed and the healing process well on its way, the crucial test was at hand. Jason was to walk on his own, without the aid of his brace, for the first time. Breathlessly, the entire staff watched as Jason swung his legs over the side of the bed. Locking his knees together, he stood, straight and tall.

Emotions ran high as nurses and doctors watched with tears of joy in their eyes. Jason had won. His life forever from that day forward would be changed.

CHAPTER 42

Father Dominic

*I*n the early days of Father Dominic Cook's priesthood, he took seriously his vow of poverty. He dressed in clerical suits of poor quality, walked to the homes of house-bound parishioners in need of Holy Communion, and strenuously fasted before Holy Days. His demeanor was one of deep humility and service to God.

When Rosa presented him with the check for $8,000, he at first refused it. Dominic later had a change of heart and by so doing a remarkable change took place. He set his sights higher, feeling deep in his heart that he could better serve mankind and become a strong voice in the church, if he were more worldly.

Gone now were the threadbare suits and ragged coat. In their place were suits of fine black broadcloth and a wool topcoat of plush cashmere. A black fedora and handsome leather shoes completed his ensemble. With his new finery, an exhilarating feeling of confidence replaced the old humility. His sermons took on more fire and brimstone and soon he began to have a following of parishioners who came to listen spellbound. He made a striking figure on the pulpit.

He had inherited Paolo's broad-shouldered physique, his father's dark hair and striking blue eyes. Father Dominic Cook's good looks and new dynamic personality did not go unnoticed. A middle-aged widow, Stella D'Orio, had attended Mass celebrated by Father Dominic for the past three months. She began mentally devising ways to begin a friendship with this handsome priest.

Unfortunately, or fortunately, whichever way you care to view the situation, she had fallen on the ice and broke her ankle. She was unable to attend Mass and called the Rectory requesting Father Dominic Cook bring her communion. She had been quite specific she wanted Father Cook and not Father Lyons, the pastor.

Stella's contributions to the church had been more than generous and Father Lyons did not wish to offend such an important parishioner. Funds were hard to come by at St. Patrick's. The community consisted mostly of middle-income families, Stella D'Orio was perhaps one of the wealthiest women in the city, having been left a sizable fortune by her late husband.

The source of his income was a mystery and Father Lyons was not one to look a gift horse in the mouth. He had been grateful the widow had chosen his church as the object of her generosity. Therefore, he was not offended when her call had come in for Father Cook to bring her communion. The young man had been preaching to a full house on Sundays and Father Lyons was quick to notice the rise in the collection box. More power to him, he thought.

When Father Dominic arrived at the D'Orio mansion, he was quite surprised to find such opulence in a common neighborhood. The palatial home stood on a hill overlooking the city. A winding drive led up to an imposing and massive hand-carved oak door. A young girl, dressed in a starched, maid's uniform opened the door at his knock.

He was shown into a parlor that took his breath away. The room was done entirely in white, from deep Persian rugs to sumptuous divans with dozens of white fluffy pillows scattered over them. A huge fireplace of white stone extended one entire side of the room. A glowing fire had been set, casting the room a lovely rosy glow. Seated near the fire in a white velvet chaise lounge sat Stella, dressed in a pale pink robe.

Stella was not a beauty, but her wealth had made her a handsome woman. Her hair was always neatly coiffed and she wore only the finest gowns becoming to her figure. Her skin had been given the luxury of daily facials and her face glowed in the firelight. She was aware of the striking appearance she presented, with her white room as a back drop.

A dish of bright fresh strawberries was laid out on a glass table beside her chaise lounge. A silver coffee pot and two china cups were set out also, indicating her desire for Father Dominic to join her in a cup of coffee and some dessert, after he had given her communion.

Stella was adept at drawing out conversation from Father and before long he was telling her of his dreams for the parish: A program for the elderly; a group of volunteers to seek out the unfortunate people of the parish and collect food to be distributed among them; a young people's group; and last but certainly not least, he wanted to organize a yearly festival, the proceeds of which would go towards the purchase of a grand organ for the church.

Stella was a careful listener and it was then she secretly vowed she and Father Dominic Cook would be the activists of the church; she would be the power behind the man. We will go places, you and I, she mused. You will become Monsignor Cook and I will be your patroness. They both had one thing in common, they aspired to lofty heights. Little did they know of the pitfalls before them.

Father Dominic had been saddened when he received the news from his mother of Paul's unfortunate accident. He dedicated a Mass to the young nephew he hardly knew, feeling deep in his heart Gloria and Vincenzo had brought this tragedy upon themselves; they had turned their backs on their religion and the will of God. Their marriage had failed. He would not feel compassion for his brother Vincenzo.

Father Cook became a frequent visitor to the grand house on the hill. Together, he and Stella worked towards their magnificent plan to make St. Patrick's parish one to be admired and envied by all in the diocese. Soon parishioners from surrounding parish-es were begging to be accepted into St. Patrick's parish. Sunday Masses overflowed with the religious and two buses were added to accommodate the crowds.

The Festival, held the following fall, was a monetary success and a down-payment was made on a magnificent pipe organ. Stella wanted only the finest and demanded the largest organ east of Chicago to be installed. She then brought to St. Patrick's, at her own expense, one of the greatest organists in the eastern states. People came from all of Youngstown to listen to music that seemed to come from Heaven. The Sunday collections became so large it took four ushers to count it on Sunday afternoons.

The Archdiocese in Cleveland began to sit-up and take notice. Who was this Father Dominic Cook and how had he succeeded where Father Lyons had failed? An influential contributor had made an appearance at the Archdiocese and requested Father Cook be made a Monsignor. In light of his accomplishments, this request was taken with grave consideration.

The announcement that Father Cook had been nominated to become a Monsignor had reached St. Joseph's Church and Father Andrew waxed eloquent over the many accomplishments his protegé had rendered over his years at St. Patrick's. No formal invitations were given out, but on the glorious day, St. Patrick's was filled to overflowing.

A small, white-haired lady sat quietly in the back of the church when the announcement was made from the pulpit. Let him be happy, she murmured to herself. May God guide him on the right path. She went unnoticed by the horde of well-wishers who pressed forward to shake his hand.

Monsignor Cook had taken to eating many of his dinners with Stella. They had developed a camaraderie that belied Stella's true feelings. She was filled with desire and found herself dreaming of him, naked before her. He had never touched her but in her wild imagination, she could feel his hands over her body.

One particularly humid evening after they had finished dinner, Monsignor Cook removed his suit jacket, hanging it on the back of his chair. He walked to the open French doors hoping to get a breath of fresh air. From her chair Stella sat watching his well-formed body move quietly. His slim hips, like that of a younger man, set her pulses racing. She came up behind him and when he turned unexpectedly, they were only inches apart. Her body ached for him and she threw her arms about his neck and kissed him passionately on the lips. He pulled away from her, horrified.

She had expected surprise, even indignation, but his face had been filled with utter revulsion. She ran from the room in shame and could hear the front door slam shut as he hastily departed. In the safety of her room she splashed cold water on her burning cheeks. His actions had spoken louder than words. A startling revelation became apparent to her: He hated women! Stella could hardly believe the sordid discovery the past hour had revealed and her part of it.

Dominic had fled from the mansion, filled with hate for the woman who would have defiled him. All his life he had fought the enemy within him. As a young boy, he had smothered his unnatural feelings for his baby brother, Vincenzo. He had never touched Vincenzo in any way but a brotherly fashion, but when the young lad was in his teens, Dominic was filled with torment.

His flight into the seminary, which he believed was to be his sanctuary instead became a prison from which he knew no escape. His contact with young men drove him to further frustration. It was here he committed his first and only indiscretion. Confession to his Father Confessor at the seminary absolved him of his heinous crime. From that day forward he had led a celibate life.

He knew Stella was not a stupid woman, she was sure to guess his secret. His mind was in a turmoil. He drove around the city for hours, not knowing where to turn. I must have an audience with Archbishop Cummings, he thought. I can rely on his good judgment. He drove all night trying to sort out his thoughts and by dawn's early light found himself in Cleveland. He hastened to the Chancery Office where the Archbishop maintained his offices.

Archbishop Cummings was taken by surprise when his secretary informed him that Monsignor Cook was waiting to see him. He listened attentively to the harried man before him. He was to learn only of Stella's behavior. The Monsignor had led a celibate life and now temptation had been thrust upon him by a trusted friend and parishioner.

He was incapable of knowing how to deal with the situation. It was obvious the Monsignor was deeply upset and Archbishop Cummings was filled with compassion. He was aware of the Monsignor's splendid record; the Church needed men of such capabilities.

"We will help you, my son," he answered gravely.

And so it was decided Monsignor Dominic Cook would take a sabbatical to Rome, where he would remain, under the protective canopy of the Vatican.

Part Five:

The End of An Era

Chapter 43

When Christina was well enough to travel, Damien bundled her up and carried her to the car. Maria and Jason sat waiting. The trip home was a joyous one. She and Jason occupied the back seat where they sat, his arm about her, their faces wreathed in smiles. Frankie and Rosa had returned home the week before where all was in readiness for the happy return of Christina.

Christina's convalescence encompassed a lengthy period of six months. It was obvious to the officers of the Metropolitan she would never be strong enough to honor her contract. They graciously terminated their agreement with a great deal of regret. She could have become a great star.

Christina relinquished her dream of an operatic career with a faint feeling of relief. Her only desire now was to become Mrs. Jason Stone. This dream came true the following September when she and Jason received the sacrament of Holy Matrimony at St. Joseph's Church, with the entire family in attendance.

Frankie had graduated from college years before and had entered into Vincenzo's architectural firm as an apprentice. After two years he became restless. He had always been a gregarious person and loved being with people. When it became apparent Americans were falling in love with the automobile, he decided he would like to open an agency of his own. Youngstown had no Ford agency at that time. The initial outlay for such an endeavor was three hundred dollars.

He had no money and could not get up enough courage to ask Damien for a loan. Going to Rosa he laid out his plan. "Grandma, would you invest in a car agency with me?"

Rosa still had several thousand dollars in the bank and could easily afford the three hundred dollars. "Are you sure that's what you want, Frankie?"

"Yes, Grandma. The auto industry will skyrocket someday," he answered excitedly.

"Then you may have the money. Have you obtained the rights yet?"

"I have an appointment with one of the managers tomorrow."

"Good! Let me know the outcome. You can take me to the bank and I will withdraw the money."

Frankie was elated and danced a little jig around Rosa, kissing her as he did so. The Cook Agency opened two months later, with Frankie the proud owner.

When Jason and Christina had been married one year, they joined him, engaging in the management of the business. Of course, Jason still painted, but the security the auto dealership afforded he and Christina enabled him to be all the more free and creative with his art.

The loan Rosa had made was paid off in the first year with interest. Frankie was a terrific automobile salesman, a position he was deeply proud to proclaim. The Cook Agency sponsored baseball teams, providing uniforms for the young boys in poor neighborhoods. He had found his niche in the world.

It is said that on October 24, 1929, a volcano erupted on the floor of the New York Stock Exchange. It burned corporations, banks, taxi drivers, farmers, janitors, chorus girls, and all those who had been riding high in the final triumph over poverty. Blocks of shares went down the drain in ten- and twenty-thousand lots. Big traders and bankers were not able to stop the flood.

The torrent of liquidation was caused by legions of small-timers who had no margins. The 1929 stock market was a mountain of credit on a molehill of real money. At that time, a person could buy a one-dollar stock with ten cents. Unemployment continued to soar and one of the primary villains were rumors, on and off the exchange. Thousands of foreign investors sold their portfolios and reinvested at home as their countries recovered from WWI.

Nowhere was the going so bad as in the idle factories. Three months after the crash men were warming their hands before scrap-wood fires. But the Great Depression was not just a blow to the extremes of millionaires and coal miners, it hurt everyone except the very poor, they had nothing to lose. Auto manufacturers let half their workers go, skyscrapers lacked tenants and a secretary was a luxury.

Truckers had nothing to truck and milk went undelivered to people who couldn't afford it. President Herbert Hoover tried to use the power of his office to expand federal construction to create new jobs. He called upon the forty-eight governors to speed up their own public works program. Henry Ford met with President Hoover at the White House and surprised other business leaders by announcing that he would give his workers a raise.

In the midst of the Depression, the Empire State Building began to be constructed. It was being hailed as a gesture of confidence and it was to be the world's tallest structure.

Frankie managed to keep afloat with his auto agency. He vacated his bachelor apartment and moved into the big house with Jason and Christina. It was a happy arrangement, he came and went as he pleased using a back entrance.

Damien and Vincenzo were stable, never having invested in the stock market. Vincenzo kept as few carpenters as he could afford, and only those who had no family were let go. Maria closed the art studio, buyers of art were too scarce. The Cook family were survivors, yet ever mindful to the plight of others. Vincenzo set up a soup kitchen in an abandoned warehouse where he, Frankie, Damien and Maria fed the needy. It was a sad era for America, yet families clung together knowing America would survive as it always had.

Chapter 44

*I*t had been a strange day. Rosa awakened early as usual. But this day she seemed listless and melancholy, a feeling foreign to her. When she went into the dining room she thought she smelled pipe smoke, the Prince Albert brand Paolo always used. She went from room to room, expecting to find someone. Dismayed, she sat in Paolo's easy chair by the fireplace, and gazed up at the lovely painting of the Italian garden. Paolo's roses seemed to bend towards her and she sat up with a start.

"I must get hold of myself," she muttered aloud. Sighing heavily, she began to make an attempt to busy herself in the kitchen. Perhaps I'll bake a pie and take it over to Christina and Jason for their dinner. As a child Christina had always loved her apple pies. But the street cars were not running any more due to the hard times. Why not cook a whole meal for them and why not invite Maria and Damien?

Eagerly, she phoned Christina and Maria, inviting them to dinner. The preparations would keep her busy and that was what she needed most of all. Christina was delighted. She had not seen her grandmother for several weeks, even though she lived only two miles away. It was difficult for her to walk that far; the bout with pneumonia had left her with little energy. She never seemed to regain her old strength. Maria and Damien would pick up Christina and Jason on the way to Rosa's.

Rosa had purchased a fresh roasting chicken the day before. "Thank goodness for ice-boxes!" she exclaimed to herself. What a convenience it was to have an ice man pass by three times a week. She could keep her supplies fresh and needed to walk to the store only once or twice during the week. Perhaps, one day, I will have an electric refrigerator, such as I have seen advertised.

Maria came by every week bringing her mother dry-goods supplies. Rosa loved to walk the two blocks to the butcher shop. She was very particular about the cuts of meat and chickens she purchased; she had a sharp eye and an even sharper nose for she could spot a bad piece of beef or an old chicken immediately.

Rosa made a savory stuffing, rich in eggs. She hummed a little song as she stuffed the chicken and rubbed the outer skin generously with butter. The potatoes were cut and peeled and placed in cold water. The apple pie was bubbling away in the oven, and Rosa set about cleaning the string beans.

Standing at the kitchen sink, she gazed out the wide window that overlooked the garden. For a split second she thought she saw two small children playing in the yard. Startled, she drew herself up sharply. Her mind was playing tricks on her and she suddenly became very weary. She hoped the family would arrive early. She could take a short nap while the chicken was in the oven. Dinner was to be at 6 p.m. She heard the car drive up at five and was relieved. Now she could lie down for half an hour, Maria would look after the meal.

"Mama, everything smells so good!" Maria exclaimed as she kissed her mother fondly.

"My favorite restaurant is right here, Mama Cook," joked Damien.

Maria noted her mother's tired face and spoke kindly, "Mama, why don't you lie down for a spell? I'll call you when everything is ready."

"Thank you, dear. I was hoping you would say that," smiled Rosa.

Going to her bedroom, she stood before Paolo's photograph, gazing up into his strong, handsome face and spoke to him as she had habitually done lately.

"I miss you so, Paolo. But it is comforting to know you are

waiting for me." Then reaching far back into her dresser drawer, she brought out a worn, white cloth which she now unwrapped. There lay the remnants of the pressed red rose Paolo had given her all those years ago. Bringing it to her cheek, she could almost smell its sweet fragrance and she re-lived the magical moment.

Then carefully wrapping it again, she placed it gently back in its place. Taking up her beloved crucifix, she lay down upon the bed planning to rest before dinner. She had grown extremely tired now and an hour later, when Christina came in to call her for dinner, the anguished girl found Rosa in her eternal sleep with the lovely crucifix still in her hand.

This is not the end of Paulo and Rosa's story for they live on in their children and grandchildren and great-grandchildren. Vincenzo built hundreds of sturdy homes throughout Ohio, all of which still stand today. Philomena's husband, James Saunders, became a U.S. Senator and she was an active partner in his campaign. Maria and Damien founded a school for underprivileged children, naming it the Cook Foundation in memory of Rosa and Paolo. Monsignor Dominic Cook remained in Rome. Christina and Jason, although childless, were a loving aunt and uncle to Frank, Jr.'s five children.

Rosa and Paolo's love affair spanned fifty-nine years, until Rosa took her last breath, and was unique in its completely unselfish devotion. Their delight in one another surpassed most commitments made by husbands and wives today. Each thought only of the other, wanting simply a shared happiness. The legacy they left their children was the opportunity to have been a part of that beautiful relationship, which they carry over into their own lives and they will share its warmth and love for generations to come.

Author's Biography

Rita Louise Monaco was born in Youngstown, Ohio in 1921, one of six children, of whom five survived. Her little brother Alberto died of pneumonia at two-and-a-half years; she remembers her sorrow, and the small white casket in the parlor. Rita's mother was a devoted wife, loving and dutiful, a good cook and home-maker. Her father was trained from eight years old as a tailor in Italy and was re-  spected and beloved in America by all who knew him. There was always singing and dancing in their home, hearty food, and lots of stories. Rita listened to the old people and cared about their stories, which can be told now, since they are all gone and beyond caring about truth or lies.

Rita writes about her family, what she heard sitting at the sup-per table, or while hiding at the top of the stairs as the grown-ups whispered. Here begins Rita's legacy as a Storyteller and keeper of family history that will be passed on to new and forever gener-ations.

At 95 years old, Rita will say she has lived a rich life. She was married 56 years to the man who won her heart by taking her dancing to Glenn Miller in the moonlight. She cannot help but sing whenever music is played, and if she doesn't know the words, she will hum. A devout Catholic and a traditional good mom to three children, she wore many hats: troop leader, festival volun-teer and organizer of church events. She is still a celebrator of baptisms, communions, marriages and funerals.

Rita moved in 1947 to West Hollywood, California, the land of endless summer and movie stars. A grandmother, great-grandmother and great-great-grandmother, she lives independently in California's Central Valley where she still enjoys cooking, knitting, writing and reading, as she always has. Rita is currently at work on her memoir, *Growing Up Italian.*

Rita Louise Monaco and Janis Monaco Clark

Mother & Daughter
Legacy Series

Turtle Moon Publishing is pleased to invite submission of Legacy Life Stories. When women's stories are told inter-generationally, mother to daughter to grandchild, from one or all perspectives, the world will be a much richer place. As described in *Nine Passages for Women and Girls: Ceremonies and Stories of Transformation,* the Elders have a task to share themselves with their families and create a Legacy. Live long in the hearts of those you love deeply: Keep the flame burning.

Petals from a Rose

www.ingramcontent.com/pod-product-compliance
Lightning Source LLC
Chambersburg PA
CBHW060430180626
46817CB00007B/2743